FIREWORKS

A STORY OF MURDER, GREED, AND BETRAYAL

ALISTAIR NEWTON

"IF HE DESERVED TO DIE, THEN IT'S NOT MURDER!"

Windward Publishing Company
Berkley, Massachusetts 02779

ISBN 13:978-0-9788424-1-3

Printed in the United States of America

Orders: www.alistairnewton.com

PROLOGUE

"Most people think it's fun to watch things go boom. That's because they've never seen the real thing. You'll know what I mean before you leave here. Welcome to Viet Nam gentlemen..."
—Captain Oswald Mathew Thornton, 1972 Da Nang.

The note from Judith Sullivan, my ex-mother-in-law, said:
"Come to the 4th of July party. Bring a friend and stay for the fireworks."
Judith

It was written on fancy embossed card stock and smelled of that very expensive French perfume she had made especially for her by a supplier in Paris.

This was the first time in five years after the divorce that I had been invited to the family party. You see, I had suddenly become respectable because I scored big last year on a case involving insurance fraud and murder and I used my ten percent commission to set up trust funds for the ex-wife and children. That's what happens when you're married to money. It opens a lot of doors.

The problem is I don't like fireworks. They hurt my ears and they're not funny. I've seen the real thing and believe me it's not fun to watch things go boom. So, there I was at the Sullivan's 4th of

July bash with my lady friend, Connie Wilson, mingling among the hoity-toity upper crusties of the world, wondering why I'd come. We were gathered on the patio in front of the house, a French provincial, facing west with north and south carriage house wings overlooking the river at Croton-on-Hudson.

The guest list was a power broker's dream, right out of Who's Who, comprised of actors, authors, politicians, corporate presidents, generals, admirals, diplomats, and more. They came in on their jets, landing at Westchester County Airport, and then they took the shuttle helicopters Jack Sullivan had leased, landing at the estate's small runway running adjacent to the tennis courts on the ridge behind the main house. Jack had accumulated a great amount of wealth as an international banker, and he was highly respected by everyone who knew him. We were still friends and I enjoyed his company whenever we got together.

Problem was, I didn't fit into this crowd and they never let me forget it. That was about to change forever, however, but I didn't know it at the time. You see, the problem with rich and powerful people is they don't know how to protect themselves. They hire brains and muscle to do all that and when things really get tough, they are sitting ducks. Sometimes the fates conspire to make things happen and this was about to be one of those times.

I'm William Thackery O'Keefe. I'm an insurance investigator and I don't like fraud and I don't like phonies, but there's one thing I really don't like and that's an insurance company that steals a man's money and then kills people to cover its tracks. That's not nice, but first, let me tell you what happened and then you'll understand what I'm talking about.

CHAPTER ONE

CONNIE SQUEEZED MY ARM and whispered in my ear. "You don't like crowds do you, Tiger," she said.

"These people remind me of a flock of seagulls in a feeding frenzy. They're all competing for the same prize."

"Why do you say that, they don't seem to be fighting over the food," she said.

"No, it's power and money they fight over. They're here to make sure nobody gets ahead of them."

"But you don't care about those things, so what's the problem?" she said.

"I was doing alright when we arrived until Judith began to introduce me to the other guests. 'This is the grandchildren's father,' she said. 'His name is Bill and he's in the insurance business.' "

"So, what's wrong with that? It's true, you used to be in the insurance business," Connie said.

"Yes but why couldn't she just say, 'This is William Thackery O'Keefe, the famous insurance investigator who has solved many interesting and notable cases in the last few years: the most recent being that terrible mess down there in East Harbour out on Long Island where they were killing people to get their life insurance. He busted up the whole mob and took a hefty ten percent for himself, gave it all to Natalie and the kids in trust funds and now we're talking to him again.' No, instead, she says I'm in the insurance business. People think I'm selling insurance. No wonder they all walk away and ignore me. Even the children are showing signs of confusion. See, here comes my twelve year old, Timothy."

"Dad? What the hell am I supposed to say to people?" he asked.

"I don't know, Timmy. What's the problem? And don't let your grandmother hear you swear."

"Well, Dad, Senator Cantrelli's fat, ugly daughter just asked me what my father does so I used that garbage Grandma Judith said to say about you being in the insurance business, and she said according to her father you kill people for a living. What am I supposed to say to that? Her father is a senator. He shook the President's hand at breakfast last week."

"Tell her I only kill people who need killing and I don't do it for a living. Then ask her how her father voted on the war in Iraq and ask her how many people were killed because of his vote?"

"Hey, man, that's a good one. Yeah! Thanks, Dad." He ran off, his light blond hair flopping in the breeze and reflecting the rays of the afternoon sun as he disappeared into the crowd.

"You're going to regret that," said Connie. "Big, important people don't like being made fun of."

"Neither do little unimportant guys like me. Senator Cantrelli is a two-bit low life who left Brooklyn just in time to avoid the Federal Crime Task Force investigations. He got elected with the help of his old mob friends and a lot of money that nobody can account for. I could say nastier things about his family tree but I've decided to be nice and not cause trouble today. Besides, this is a boring party with a lot of dull, boring, rich people."

"Well, dearest," she said, snuggling up against me. "It won't be dull very long. Here comes the enemy and he doesn't look happy."

Victor Cantrelli was headed my way with Judith trailing right behind him. Cantrelli's daughter was standing off to one side crying, her mother holding her by the hair, yelling in her face in another language. Timmy stood at a distance with a stricken look on his face. I gave him a quick wink to let him know it was all right and faced Cantrelli as he came to an abrupt stop inches from my nose yelling so loud everyone stopped what they were doing and stared at us.

"You low-life ambulance chasing jerk! I oughta have you thrown outta here and this blond slut with ya," he said jabbing a thumb at Connie.

"Keep it cool, Victor. You have enough troubles in your life without adding me to your list." He blinked in surprise and stepped back.

"You got no right to tell my daughter that I'm a mass murderer like Hitler. I want you to apologize to my wife and kids." At that point, Judith stepped between us.

"That will be quite enough, boys." She pushed Victor back a step and placed a hand on my chest and tried the same with me but I didn't move, and my six foot, one hundred ninety-five pounds made it necessary for both Judith and Victor to give way and step back.

"Victor," I said. "You don't want to start with me. I'm no threat to you but if you don't watch your mouth, I'll become your worst nightmare. Do you read me, Senator?" I said it with a smile, staring him straight in the eyes.

"I got friends that'll handle anything I start," he said. "You just stop telling my kids things they got no business hearing."

"Ditto to you, friend." I braced myself for an attack.

"Okay...Okay...that will do," said Judith. "That will be quite enough. I'm sure there's a simple misunderstanding here." She glanced at me, "Please, Bill, apologize. We don't need this."

"I'll do it for you and Jack." She looked relieved. "Victor, I'm sorry if I said anything about you that isn't true, okay?" I said, relaxing my fists.

"Yeah, sure, okay." He started to go.

"Just a moment, Victor. I don't care what you say about me but you owe my friend Connie an apology...So, apologize!"

"Yeah, okay, so…I'm sorry about that, Miss ahh...it was a cheap shot. I shoulda never said that, okay?" He glanced at me and I nodded.

"It's all right, Senator." Connie smiled sweetly. "I'm surprised you know me so well. We'll just chalk it up as one of life's growth experiences." The girl had a sense of humor.

"Yeah, right...ahh Forget it!" He turned and walked away.

"You certainly have a way of attracting trouble, William." Judith glared at me. "Why did you ever say those things to a United States

Senator?"

"He didn't, Mrs. Sullivan." Connie answered before I could open my mouth. "He didn't say anything like that. I think someone is playing a joke on the good senator."

"Yes, of course. I should have known...Well if you can avoid any further trouble, William, please do. The situation is bad enough dealing with the Senate Foreign Relations Committee without calling its minority leader a Hitler. You're not funny, William. I don't know why I ever thought you might have changed. I should have known better."

She turned on her heels and trooped off. I watched her go, thinking how difficult it must be to live with someone so perfect. Then I remembered that I had done just that when married to her daughter and it wasn't a pleasant life.

"Penny for your thoughts, Tiger." Connie nudged my arm.

"Oh, just remembering how tough these people can be. I'm sorry we came here."

"You like lots of room and when someone crowds you, things get sticky. I admire your restraint with Victor Cantrelli."

"It took a lot not to punch him out but it was worth it to see him back down. Tell you what. Let's get out of here."

"But Bill, what about the fireworks? You promised the children you would watch the fireworks with them."

"I don't like fireworks. Natalie and Judith know that. I've seen all the fireworks I'll ever want to see. Besides, they hurt my eyes and ears. These people think it's fun to watch things go boom."

"Okay, but let's make the best of it for now. The reason we're here is to spend time with your children."

She was right. I cared less about the rest of these people. Not one of them could protect themselves in an emergency, including the great Senator Victor Cantrelli. I thought of the 9mm Glock 17 strapped to my left ankle with two spare clips. It held seventeen rounds, an awesome weapon in a firefight. I started wearing it full time a year ago since my last case. Judith was right, I had a habit of making enemies of very powerful people. Trouble had a way of finding me so I was taking no chances.

"Let's circulate a little," said Connie. "I want to see what really makes the rich and famous tick."

"Money and power are the key words," I answered. "If you want to see these people lather up and drool at the mouth, just talk money, but make it in the millions. Anything less is considered common and boring."

"Don't let's be bitter, Mr. O'Keefe. I'm just curious."

"Me too, let's have some fun." I took her hand and we strolled off into the crowd.

CHAPTER TWO

I KNEW SOME OF THE guests so I introduced Connie and we caught up on current events. The five waiters and two barmen caught my attention as we circulated. They were all dressed the same: white shirts, black bow ties, black Huggre pants with alligator belts and shoes. Belt buckles were heavy silver and each man was short and dark with a close-cropped G.I. style haircut. I decided they were probably just migrant workers making money while working for a catering outfit. The irony struck me that if they were illegal and did not have green cards and valid visas, there were many guests at this party that were responsible for enforcing the laws that were being broken.

We walked across the tennis courts and up to the landing strip on the hill. Timmy and my youngest, eight year old Jonathan came tagging along behind us. Ten-year old Samantha didn't come. She stayed with her grandmother and pretended to be busy. Jonathan said it wasn't her choice...out of the mouths of babies.

"Wow, look at that awesome chopper." Jonathan found everything awesome. He was at an awesome age.

"That's a Bell UA-1," I said. "It holds five people, goes 160 mph, has a service ceiling of 16,500 feet and a max cruise range of 600 plus miles."

"Wow! Awesome, Dad." I felt like a million dollars. There's nothing like impressing your son in front of your girlfriend.

"Yes, I know something about helicopters. I've been in a few," and I left it at that, grateful to see Jack Sullivan coming our way.

Jonathan was irrepressible. "Hey, Gramps, Dad knows all about helicopters. He's flown in them. Did you know that?"

"I'm not surprised. Good to see you, Bill. How's it going?" We shook hands.

"Great Jack, how's it with you?" He was in excellent shape for a man of his age and his grip was as strong as ever. He had been Chairman of the World Bank, an advisor to three presidents, and an expert on international economics and had served in some of the top banks in the country before his retirement.

"I'm doing better than ever, Bill. I wish I had another lifetime to do all the things I haven't yet tried. Know what I mean? Like you, I wish I could just go off someplace, spend time alone, think pure thoughts and dream up new projects but they won't let me retire."

"What makes you think I ever do the pure thoughts routine?"

"Oh yes, Billy, I know you. You spend time out there on the Island in your cottage overlooking the Sound or sailing in your boat and you clear the cobwebs out of your brain and think clear, pure thoughts. That's why you see things differently from the rest of the world. You do what you want. You're a free spirit."

"What can I say? You got me pegged, Jack. "

"Well, according to Victor Cantrelli, you've said it all. He's minority leader on the Senate Foreign Relations Committee. He's here because I need him on a project I'm working on," he said.

"Look…ahh…Jack, I'm sorry if I messed something up. Yeah, I did go a little too far but I didn't say all those things. I don't know how it got so out of control. I was just having a little fun, you know?"

"I understand fully, Victor is a jerk that got elected but he's powerful and I need his influence in Congress to get some things done. I have to tell you, he's tricky. Half the time when I'm talking to him, I don't know if he's all there. Like he's there but he isn't, know what I mean?" Jack said.

"I'm sorry, I couldn't resist. I'll play it cool from now on. He was just too easy." I said.

"I know what you mean. I can't tell you what's going on. It's big, very, very big and I appreciate your understanding."

"It's my fault," Timothy spoke up from behind me. "I'm sorry, Gramps. It was my fault. I told Lizza Cantrelli her father voted to kill a lot of people in Iraq and she went ballistic. She's the one who said I called her father a mass murderer and a Hitler but I never said that. I'm sorry, Dad, I guess I caused a lot of trouble."

We looked at Timothy. Even at the age of twelve, he was ready to stand up and take the heat, a young man beyond his years.

"No, you didn't cause it, son. It happened because some people are just plain ignorant."

I put my hand on the back of his neck, pulled him closer and gave him a hug. He resisted at first and then put his arms around me and returned the hug. We were silent for a while as we walked along the ridge of the hill with Connie and the boys lagging behind.

"You lengthened your runway, Jack, and that looks like a brand new twin Beech in a new hanger. Are you going into the aviation business full time?"

I'm just improving the operation so I can get in and out at night and during bad weather. I have a forty-five hundred foot runway with lights. The new airplane goes higher and faster. Gives me more versatility. Used to be I would drive to Kennedy. Now I can go out of Boston, Bradley, Montreal or even Philadelphia. I can meet with people in Washington and be home for dinner with no more overnights. Wish I had those options years ago when I was younger. I spent too much of my time away from the family and most of it was traveling."

"Things change, Jack. We learn as we go."

"Yes, and some of us get a second chance. I envy you, my friend. Don't let Connie slip away. Fireworks will be starting soon. You're staying, aren't you?"

"Yes, I'll stick it out." The sun was low over the western hills as we began walking to the main house, a gentle breeze in our faces. We were headed down the hill toward the back of the house. I followed Jack and Connie was behind us with the boys.

"Say, Jack, where did you find those waiters with the tight pants and alligator shoes?" I asked.

"I don't know. Judith called the caterers and they took care of the rest. Why, any complaints?"

"No, but they don't fit. Nobody wears alligator shoes anymore, especially Latino waiters at a Westchester party."

"It's the Fourth of July, Billy. Give it up and enjoy it. Take a break. You don't have to be on duty today."

"Sorry, I'm just an old hound dog looking for the scent."

"Ha, Ha, Ha," Jack slapped me on the shoulder. "You're more like a tiger than a hound dog and I'm glad you're here. It's refreshing to talk to a real man for a change instead of all these high rollers."

We walked down to the back of the house. Jack had done it up right with an architect and a builder right from France. The view was awesome, as Jonathan would say, with Bear Mountain to the north, the Adirondacks to the west outlined in the setting sun, the Hudson River below and the Croton Reservoir over the ridge to the east. There was an old-fashioned glassed-in greenhouse off the back of the house where he spent much of his spare time raising vegetables and flowers.

"Come inside and look at my latest project," Jack said, as we approached the greenhouse.

"I've been having problems with aphids for quite awhile so I sent away for this special breed of spider that is supposed to take care of the problem. There, you can see one right under that pipe."

"Yeah, it looks like a Black Widow. Is that what it is?" I said.

"It's not supposed to be but it turns out they sent me the wrong kind and the darn things spread into the main house and both wings. We had to call in the exterminators and then we had to replace the rugs and most of the furniture because of the poison they used. Judith was impossible to live with until it was all over. Now, they're coming back out here so I guess I'll have to call the exterminator in again. I can't do that sort of spraying anymore. It gets in my lungs and I can't breath."

"Did you go back to the supplier about this?" I asked.

"Yes, and they offered to send me the right kind of spider to make up for their mistake. I told them to forget it. So, they offered me some Lady Bugs that are supposed to be good for this sort of thing. I told them no, I'll stick to my regular sprays from now on."

"Your roses look good this year, Jack. You should enter them in the state fair. Judith would be proud of you."

"Wish I could. Maybe I'll take a break after this deal is over. I'll need it even if everything goes well." He looked at me with a troubled expression I hadn't seen since my divorce from his daughter.

"It's the biggest deal of my entire life. If I pull it off, I'll be the king of the international financial world." We started out the door of the greenhouse and around the front of the main house.

"If you need a friend, just call," I said. I wanted to say more but Connie and the boys had caught up and were tagging along right behind us.

"Thanks, I may just do that." A faint smile crossed his face.

"Look at the fireworks," Jonathan yelled. "Awesome! Come on, let's go, Dad. Come on Tim." They were off before I could say, 'Be careful.'

"I'll see you later, Bill. Spend time with your kids." We shook hands and parted. Jack moved away, his shoulders sagging as if he were suddenly a hundred years old.

I strolled around to the front of the house with Connie and joined the children sitting on the stone wall which surrounded the patio. The exotic bushes and shrubs, well manicured and placed artistically along the other side of the wall, gave the whole scene a secluded feeling. The fireworks went off across the front of the hill overlooking the Hudson River.

Jack had done an excellent job and the partygoers applauded as each wave of rockets went off, bigger and louder. I endured the noise and flashing shock waves of the explosions, fighting the impulse to hit the dirt and dig in until it was over. Connie helped by holding my hand. Jonathan came out with some 'wicked, awful, awesomes' while Samantha squealed and held her ears. Timothy sat erect and unblinking as a young man should. It was over before we knew it, the finale lighting up the sky with a grand display of rocket bursts and thunderous explosions shaking the ground.

"That was a big one!" Connie said as she ducked her head and squeezed my hand.

"Yeah, almost too big," I said. "I don't think the ground should have shaken that much but I'm just glad it's over." The lights came on and people started moving around. Suddenly, there was a disturbance on the other side of the patio. People were shouting and cursing as a scuffle broke out.

"How dare you..." a woman screamed.

"Damn you..." a man's voice was cut short.

"Get your hands off her!" Victor Cantrelli was yelling at one of the waiters who had hold of his wife sitting in a wicker chair. I thought this was just another Cantrelli incident and nothing out of the ordinary. Then I saw the gun the waiter was holding in his left hand as he threw a backhand slap across Victor's face, smacking him solidly across the bridge of his nose with the side of the revolver...a very effective way of subduing a man. Suddenly, a big ape of a man came charging from the shadows, reaching inside his coat jacket. He pulled a gun and tried to point it at the waiter but he was cut down by a salvo of shots before he got his weapon leveled...Victor Cantrelli's bodyguard was no more.

"Everyone will not move, pleeze!"

The headwaiter stood on a chair in the middle of the patio, an AK-47 slung carelessly under his right shoulder, his finger on the trigger. Judith Sullivan, always the efficient hostess, stepped forward and confronted him.

"Just what do you think you are doing?" she demanded, stopping squarely in front of the headwaiter's chair. I had to hand it to her, the old girl had sand.

"I am steeking you up, Senora!" he said in a heavy accent, and he pointed the AK-47 straight at the exposed cleft of her ample bosom.

CHAPTER THREE

THEY WERE QUICK. WE were surrounded, with one robber in each corner of the patio, two in front on the grass, and two guarding the house. Victor Cantrelli was coming awake again, yelling, and his wife was screaming. One of the waiters slapped her and conked Contrelli on the head. Jonathan was the first to react to the situation.

"Geeez...Wow...hey Dad, let em' have it."

"He's too chicken," Samantha sneered, shades of her mother.

"Quiet! Both of you shut up," Timothy hissed.

"Shut up yourself, dummy. You can't make me," Samantha shot back as she punched him in the shoulder.

The corner men started moving down the line, collecting jewelry and other valuables. No one resisted and I couldn't blame them. These guys were scary, even if they did have bad taste in clothes.

"Bill, what should we do?" Connie asked, grabbing my arm.

"Just play it cool for now, Babe. I'm not sure what's going on here." I said.

I tried to make sense of what was happening. This was a July Fourth picnic and there wasn't much valuable jewelry on display. There were a few expensive tennis rackets and some of the ladies' outfits cost more than a normal working man could make in a year, but not anything that could be pawned for big bucks. They should have waited for a formal ball or the Governor's tea party if they wanted to rob the guests. This much manpower and firepower was costly. It required some organization but there didn't seem to be any and I wondered how they intended to get away. One call to the local police and there would be roadblocks everywhere. There had to be something bigger than just a "steek up".

I thought of pulling the Glock from my left ankle holster but dismissed it. Not that I couldn't get it out and take two or three of them down, but there were too many innocent people in the way and one of those AK-47s could do a lot of permanent damage. My reveries were interrupted as one of the waiter-robbers stopped in front of me and thrust his pistol in my face: Big Mistake! Then he reached across with his left hand and ripped the gold locket off Samantha's neck: Bigger Mistake! It had a picture inside it of the family in happier times. I gave it to her on her fifth birthday and it meant a lot to me to see her wearing it. I stood up very slowly, my arms at my sides flexing my hands to loosen up.

"Give it back, Chico!" I whispered in his face.

"Sit down! You shut up!" He pushed the pistol hard into my stomach: Biggest Mistake! He reached across and grabbed Samantha, pulling her up next to him, and said, "Nice leetle girl." Last Mistake!

Now, there are several ways of taking a handgun away from someone. All of them are very risky. This fellow was not under control and there was no doubt in my mind he would try to kill me if he thought I was a threat. I looked him straight in his eyes, held his gaze and realized he was high on something.

"You don't want to do this, Chico. It's not worth it to die over a little girl's locket," I said.

I stared him straight in the eyes. I wanted him to concentrate on me but he was an idiot. A slow smile spread across his face and there was a perceptible tightening of the muscles in his right arm. I knew he was going to pull the trigger. I quickly placed my left hand over the top of the revolver and twisted the gun into his belly making certain to keep the cylinder from rotating. At the same moment I chopped hard at his neck with my right hand. He was small but he was in good condition and very fast. He let go of the revolver and staggered back from my blow. Then he turned and threw a back-kick at my head. He almost got me but I blocked the kick just in time and countered with one of my own, catching him on the chin. I felt the bones in his jaw give way and he went down hard on his back.

It all happened in a split second, and when I looked up the leader, still standing on the chair, was fumbling with his rifle, trying to bring it to bear on me. Evidently, he had not expected to use it because he was working the action to chamber a round: another Big Mistake. I cocked the hammer of the pistol, a cheap East German model, leveled and fired. He went backward off the chair, firing into the air as he went down. Everyone was up and running, screaming, yelling, kicking, grabbing. One of the AK-47s went off into the air as two picnickers ran over one of the robbers knocking him to the ground. I turned to Connie and found her holding Samantha, a look of terror on her face.

"Get behind the wall. Get down behind the wall, NOW!" I yelled.

I waved them back. Timothy was the first to move, grabbing Jonathan as he ducked over the stone wall and down into the evergreen shrubs. Connie was right behind with Samantha. I turned and saw one of the robbers bent over picking up his loot and I shot him twice before he could stand up. The place was emptying out fast. The last waiter disappeared around the corner of the hedge and I realized I was listening to a new noise in the distance. It was the sound of incoming helicopters. It figured. I checked behind the wall and found everyone huddled down in the dirt.

"Stay here," I yelled to Connie. "Take care of the kids." She nodded and I handed her the pistol. I pulled the Glock from its ankle holster, put the two spare clips in my pocket and charged around the hedge and across the tennis courts. The choppers were just landing. I thought I might make it after all but I was not in peak condition and a two hundred yard uphill sprint after a long day of heavy picnicking was sheer torture.

I was about half way up the slope when there was a blinding flash and I felt the concussion of an explosion, and then there was another. I instinctively ducked, lost my footing and fell flat on my face, forced myself up and kept pumping up the hill. Near the top I got the feeling I wasn't alone and I turned, pointing the Glock, only to find Timothy, wide-eyed and breathing hard, staring at the barrel of my gun, a look of terror on his face.

"I told you to stay put."

"I thought you might need help," he shouted over the roar of the helicopter engines.

"Stay behind me and keep down."

I sprinted the last few yards and saw that the area was like a war zone. The two shuttle helicopters were on fire, destroyed, and the body of one of the pilots lay nearby. There were two choppers executing the escape. One was already airborne and out of range down the runway. The second one, right in front of me, was about thirty feet away and just lifting off.

Contrary to popular opinion, it's not that easy to shoot down a helicopter, especially with a nine-millimeter semi-automatic handgun. I should have grabbed an AK-47 but there wasn't enough time. I could aim for the pilot but the curved Plexiglas would probably deflect the bullet. Even if I was lucky enough to hit him, a wounded pilot could fly a long way. We proved that one in Viet Nam. Then again, I could aim for the fuel tanks but these choppers were foreign, and I wasn't really certain where the fuel was stored.

So, I decided to aim for the engines and I fired off a clip as the last chopper rose and began its forward movement. I jammed a second clip home and emptied that at the glowing exhaust ports as it went away from me. I aimed higher and higher leading my target, hoping I would get lucky and put a slug down the stack and into the turbine blades of the jet engines, a long shot at best.

I emptied the second clip and had almost given up hope when the chopper, now in a steep left turn, suddenly lost power and began to sink out of sight down the mountain. The flames from the exhaust on the left engine went out and there was a perceptible decrease in the beat of the rotors. Then came the crash. It sounded like a bunch of cats fighting inside some trashcans, rolling around in a dark dead end alley. There was no fire, just the screeching, tearing sound of metal objects banging off the trees, rocks and solid earth of the mountain.

"Awesome!" a little voice behind me said.

I turned to find Jonathan and Samantha standing next to Timothy. Connie was running up the hill after them, an expression of terror on her face.

"What the hell are you two doing here?" I yelled.

"We thought you might need some help, Dad," said Jonathan. Samantha nodded, wide-eyed in agreement.

Connie came puffing up to us, "I'm sorry, Bill. I turned and they were gone. I can't believe how fast they are."

Oh well, like I said, the Fourth of July has always been a family affair. Eat a little, play a little, watch some fireworks, and shoot some terrorists: all in a day's work.

CHAPTER FOUR

THE SCENE WAS ONE of chaos. Both of the shuttle helicopters were burning and debris littered the runway. I stood there staring into the darkness where the helicopter full of robbers had just crashed, a feeling of despair coming over me.

"Keep these kids here," I said to Connie, and I walked over to the pilot on the ground and checked his body. He was dead, wasted by an AK-47 and not a pretty sight. I turned to find Timothy next to me, wide-eyed, his mouth agape. He would remember tonight. Fortunately, Connie managed to keep the other two away.

"Now you see why I said to stay back there, Timmy? They had real guns and real bullets. This is not play acting. It's not the movies."

He didn't answer. He just stood there, frozen. Then I regretted what I'd said. I took him in my arms and carried him down the hill with the others following behind.

The scene on the patio had not changed. The bodies of the waiters were still where they had fallen. Natalie was standing next to the one who had taken Samantha's locket, tears streaming down her cheeks with Judith next to her, a look of total dismay on her face. It has always amazed me how the rich and elite lack competency in the face of reality.

"Where have you been?" Natalie said. "I was worried sick. How could you do such a terrible thing to us, William? I hope you're satisfied because you have absolutely ruined the party and you scared me to death. I didn't know where the children were. I only knew they were gone...oh my poor babies." She scooped up Samantha as I put Timothy down.

"Well, William?" Judith was less hysterical but equally accusative. "You certainly make a very poor example of a father figure for these children. Starting a fight and running away is not the way to build character."

"You got it all wrong, Grandma." Jonathan spoke up. "Dad knocked the robber out and shot the other two guys and then he ran up the hill and shot the helicopter down. Wow, it was awesome. You should have seen it."

"Don't be ridiculous, dear. You're upset. Everything will be just fine now. Come with me." Judith reached for his arm.

Natalie took Samantha's hand and started away, expecting the other children to follow but Samantha pulled away and ran to the inert figure of the waiter on the ground. He was still breathing but he wasn't moving. She bent over and removed her locket from his hand, turned to me and pulled me down. Then she put her arms around my neck, kissed me on the cheek and gave me a big hug.

"Thanks, Dad," she said smiling, and walked off with Natalie. Jonathan followed at Judith's insistence.

"She is nuts," said Connie." She thinks this is all your doing and her mother supports that behavior."

"She personalizes everything and directs it at the source of all her anger and that's me. Her mother won't face her own failures as a parent so she supports the daughter's sickness. Let's face it, if it weren't for me, she probably wouldn't make it through the day. She just needs someone to blame."

"How did you ever live with that, Bill? You must have been a saint." She grinned.

"Believe it or not, Connie, I'm a pretty easy going guy."

"Yeah, sure, unless a sleazy Latino waiter touches your daughter's locket."

"Every man has his limits." I kicked Chico but he didn't move. A moment of regret passed over me and then I dismissed it. We do what we have to do to survive. He wanted to play with the big boys and now he knew the score.

The night was fully settled in as lights in the distant valleys and hills began winking on in households and neighborhoods far removed from the violence and death that had come to visit us there at the Sullivan estate. Stars were twinkling in the sky overhead as the moon shone brightly just above the horizon, making it a perfect Fourth of July night with a slight warming breeze. Other fireworks displays were starting up in the distance and we could see rockets shooting into the sky. The sound of a siren wafted over the night air and the flashing lights of an ambulance came round a sharp turn of the country road below, leading up to the main house. I turned to Timothy and put my hand on his shoulder.

"How're you doing, pal?" He looked at me with pleading eyes.

"I never thought it would be this way...I mean, you never really think about it, I guess, but those men...they're really dead, aren't they?" He started to cry and I gave him a hug.

"It's okay, soldier. You'll be all right. It's never easy so just be glad you're still alive and the rest will pass...eventually. They were all bad men and they deserved to die. Believe me, they would have killed us if they had the chance."

He seemed to buy it. There never has been a fixed formula for dealing with this sort of trauma. He was too young, but then I saw boys in Vietnam who were less prepared to handle the horrors of battle. Timothy had just been in his first action, seen his first enemy destroyed, and experienced the numbing trauma of death first hand. Even though he didn't pull the trigger himself, he was there and saw his father do it and now I had to stick by him.

"Do you feel bad about killing them?" he asked.

"Yes, but it's something I had to do. There was no one else to protect you guys. Unfortunately, the police can't be everywhere and when people like these start hurting innocent people, we have to fight back. They're killers and they won't listen to reason. Take that fellow on the ground right there," I pointed to Chico. "I gave him a choice to let go of Samantha or accept the consequences. He was going to pull the trigger of that pistol so I took it away from him. He tried to hurt me so I hurt him."

"Grandma Judith says we shouldn't hurt people."

"Your grandmother Judith never had to face a man with a gun knowing that he was going to kill her. Ignoring violence won't make it go away. It's one thing to bluff a guy standing on a chair and another thing when he's got you by the throat with one hand and shooting you in the belly with the other. One is an intellectual exercise while the other is survival. That's why I fought back, son. It was a matter of survival." I paused for a moment. "Can you understand that, Timothy?"

"I...yes...I think so. It makes sense. You fight back only when you have to and then you fight to win...right?"

"Right."

We were interrupted by the arrival of the ambulance and a police car. Things would get crazy now. Just at that moment Judith came out of the main house and walked toward us.

"William, can you come with me, please?" For Judith to say please was a first.

"Why, Judith? I was just spending some time with Timmy."

"I am sorry, Bill," she said looking around, "but Jack needs you. He's in very serious trouble."

CHAPTER FIVE

JUDITH NEVER SAID PLEASE, and it was almost earthshaking for her to admit that something was wrong let alone that Jack was in trouble. They were always very formal in their relations and I wondered if that behavior carried into their private lives, like the bedroom. As we walked through the house, its beauty and perfection reminded me of how tenuous life was. It could all be wiped out by the ugliness of the world in the blink of an eye. I followed Judith through the front door and turned right into the library on the south side of the house.

I smelled the nitro before we reached the breezeway to the south carriage house wing. Its distinctive smell left a latent imprint in a subterranean part of my brain from the time I'd spent in the jungles of Viet Nam. Now I was in a beautiful French provincial estate and as we entered the office I had that same old feeling that I was about to step into big trouble.

"They blew the safe, Bill. They must have done it during the finale of the fireworks," said Jack. "I can't believe someone would do a thing like this. It just doesn't make any sense."

He pointed to the wall beside the desk to the right of the French windows where the safe had been hidden behind a small tapestry, a tortured look on his face.

"What a mess," Judith said, as she put her arms around him, but he just stared at the wall. Two men stood near the desk, looking on.

He finally came back to reality. "I don't know what to say. It's more serious than you can imagine." He looked around as if lost.

"Sit down, dear, take it easy." Judith turned to me and said, "Have you met Admiral James Rassmussen?" She indicated the younger of the two men. "And this is Ambassador Malcome Kitterage." The names suddenly fit the faces. Rassmussen was the Chief of Procurement for the Navy and Kitterage was ambassador to the United Nations. A short dark man with expensive picnic duds strolled into the room and joined us. He appeared very suave but his eyes darted around the room, taking in the scene like a caged rat.

"This is Salvatore Santiago, President of the World Bank," said Judith, warming to her hostess duties. Jack, now sitting at his desk, seemed very nervous and distracted. I shook Santiago's hand and found it weak and clammy. His manor was stiff and he was shaking all over but he spoke perfect English.

"Good evening, Mr. O'Keefe. I am so glad you could be with us. I understand the robbers threatened your family; most unfortunate. It's best not to resist such people. They are less likely to overreact if you do not resist. Look what happened to poor Senator Cantrelli."

"That only works, Mr. Santiago, when no one touches your daughter." I stared into his eyes and he glanced the other way.

"Ahh, yes, how noble. Mr. O'Keefe was protecting his daughter. That makes all the difference." His hands still shook.

"Can we get on with this?" Ambassador Kitterage said impatiently. "This place will be crawling with policemen very shortly. We really haven't much time and speaking for myself, I really don't want to have my name in the newspaper tomorrow because of this unfortunate incident."

"Right!" said Jack. "Let's all sit down and relax so we can get on with it. Bill, you can sit here next to my desk."

"I'll be just outside if you need me, dear." Judith said as she made her exit and closed the door. Jack took charge.

"Gentlemen, I've asked my son-in-law, William O'Keefe, to be here. He's a trained investigator and, as you saw tonight, he's a take-charge guy. I'd like to hear his observations. Any objections?"

There was a moment of silence and then Rassmussen spoke. "I

think we should allow the FBI and INTERPOL to handle this. We can't afford any more mistakes." His gaze settled on Jack.

"Perhaps we should just wait and allow things to settle down. Frankly, I feel the need to get back to the comfort of my own home," said Ambassador Kitterage.

"I can put investigators on this case right now," Rassmussen said. "The Navy has the best intelligence network in the world. All I have to do is pick up that phone and call the President."

"I don't think we need to bother the President, gentlemen," said Kitterage.

"Don't be silly, Malcome. The President is the one who gave me the damned report. I have to notify him. That automatically brings the FBI into it, so let's not quibble. This problem requires special treatment. That's why I want O'Keefe to give us his observations. He's the best there is at what he does," said Jack.

I was flattered but Jack was full of baloney. He had something else on his mind, so I would wait for him to play it out.

"Let's get on with it." Jack turned to me. "Bill, it's not by chance that we're all here today. Admiral Rassmussen brought a report with him from the President. I haven't read it yet, but it's related to some international financial estimates and a plan to link markets through the World Bank. We were to meet tonight to discuss it after the fireworks. Someone else got there first. I don't know why. The only person not here is Senator Cantrelli. He went to the hospital with his bodyguard, who's not expected to make it."

"I can only guess at what happened here, Jack. At first it appeared to be a highly organized and very well financed operation. It was a foreign group, probably Latin American. The accents were real. The pros will identify them but the timing is all wrong. They knew everything about your party and that means inside information, but the robbery was sloppy."

"How do you arrive at such a flimsy conclusion, Mr. O'Keefe?" Santiago said, fidgeting with his wristwatch.

"Simple, Mr. Santiago. If you're going to steal expensive baubles, you don't pick a Fourth of July picnic. You find a formal ball where everyone is wearing their most expensive jewelry. There was no reason to rob the guests. They had the safe cleaned out before anyone even stood up to clear their ears. So why the robbery? The answer is obvious. They were small time hoods and the robbery was their payoff. They appeared to be paramilitary because of the weapons and helicopters, but I think they were just cheap hoods."

"You're making a lot of assumptions, are you not?" Kitterage challenged.

"That's how a case is built, Mr. Ambassador. After each assumption comes a review of the possibilities. A good investigator rechecks these every step of the way, fitting new evidence into the structure of the case as it develops. I have questions about what's happened and I'll warn you, the FBI isn't going to be easy to convince, so I hope you have your stories straight before they arrive."

"That's simple," said Santiago. "We were robbed."

"Not really, Sal. They'll want to know what was stolen and why the safe was blown," said Jack. "The report was top secret so it's our responsibility to report it. Besides, I've already called the White House and talked to the Chief of Staff, Samuel Sontaigm, so the ball is rolling. We have no choice but to cooperate with the FBI but the local police need to know only that it's a common robbery, okay?" Everyone nodded in agreement. There was a knock at the door and Judith poked her head through the opening.

"A policeman is here and he wants to see you, Jack.

"Send him in," Jack said, standing up. "Gentlemen, here we go."

Judith stepped aside and a young man with Oriental features, dressed in a red golf shirt and lime green pants, both with an alligator, stepped through the door. He was about six inches shorter than my six feet but he carried himself in a slouched position that was deceptive. His walk was that of a jungle cat, a well tuned fighting machine. I'd seen this kind before and I never underestimated them, probably black belt and more. He had a bemused smile which didn't change as he was introduced, shaking hands until he came to me.

"Deputy Sheriff Kim Woo, this is my son-in-law, Bill O'Keefe," said Jack. Woo nodded and I nodded but we didn't shake hands. We just sized each other up.

"They say you blocked a back kick and countered, dropped the waiter guy and took his pistol, dropped two more, then ran up the hill and shot down a helicopter with your pea shooter...very impressive," he said, still smiling.

"You can't always believe everything you hear," I said.

"I hear much about you. I'm thinking it may all be true."

"You're making me blush," I said, holding his gaze.

"I don't think so. Your methods are being studied at the State Police Academy because of your success in cracking that East Harbour murder conspiracy case last year. What they do is use you as an example of what not to do." The smile persisted.

"Like I said, you can't believe everything you hear...so tell me, ahh, Kim, what's a deputy sheriff doing here on a robbery call? I thought the local police would handle this one."

"They will, but this place is just outside the town limits so the county has jurisdiction. I'll do my part and they'll do theirs until the state police come in with the forensics team. Then everyone will jockey around for a piece of the action. It's always that way until a decision is made about who's in charge."

"Why don't we all sit down," said Jack. "I hate to disappoint you, Mr. Woo, but there really isn't much we can tell you. It appears we were robbed and that's about it." Woo looked around the room.

"Yes, of course, I understand. I am obviously way out of my depth here so I won't waste time with a lot of questions. I asked Mrs. Sullivan about the caterers and evidently no one knows who they were. We will find out more about them after an examination of the bodies and the helicopter. So, if there is anything you can think of that might help, I'll be happy to listen to your comments." His eyes wandered to the blown safe but he said nothing about it.

"Actually, I was about to leave if you don't mind, deputy?" said Ambassador Kitterage, standing up.

"Not at all, sir. If you need a ride, I'll be happy to arrange it."

"I'll follow you, Malcome." Salvatore Santiago started for the door ahead of everyone as we all stood and Rassmussen followed.

They said their goodbyes leaving Jack, myself, and Deputy Woo, who walked over to the wall safe and began examining the damage. He bent down and pointed at the safe's door on the floor.

"Very professional. Drilled into the dial there at the zero. Nitro injected into the mechanism and set off by remote control. See? The detonator is still stuck in the hole. Don't see that sort of work too often nowadays. Most thieves use plastique explosive because it's easier to handle, safer to carry. Even a rank amateur can set the stuff off but it doesn't do as good a job. Nitro is different, requires a real pro. Not many safe crackers around who still use the stuff so it shouldn't be too difficult to round up a few suspects on this one."

"I'm impressed, Deputy Woo." I knew something about safes and cracking them but Woo had it all over me. The telephone rang and Jack answered it.

"Yes, I understand. Thank you." He hung up. "That was the FBI in Washington. The forensics team is on its way in a Lear jet. They're estimating Westchester County Airport in thirty minutes. They'll break off their approach and come in here. They just wanted to make certain the airstrip is clear and that the runway lights will be on."

Woo looked puzzled. "You say the FBI is coming in here? Is there something I don't know, Mr. Sullivan?"

"You might as well know, Mr. Woo. There were government documents in that safe and that evidently was the reason for the robbery. I can't tell you more than that but if we don't recover them and stop whoever took them, it could mean the end of everything. I'm sorry but I cannot tell you anything more than that and I must ask you not to tell anyone what we have discussed."

I looked at Woo and he looked at me and we both looked at Jack. I'd kept my cool up till now waiting for Jack to clear up what was happening, but I wasn't prepared for the "end of everything."

"Well, I suppose I'll read about it in the history books. If you need me, I'll be around…ahh…investigating and...well, whatever," Woo said and he smiled at me, shook Jack's hand and went out.

Jack sat down at his desk, his head bowed like a defeated man. I poured two slugs of Old Barlow's Tennessee Sour Mash Whiskey and sat next to the desk.

"Here's lookin' at you, Jack," I said, trying to be jovial. We both put it down and I poured two more.

"Now Jack, tell me the truth. What is really going on? I like to know where the alligators are before I start swimming across the swamp."

"I was overly dramatic there for a moment but I guess I wasn't far wrong. If that report gets out, all hell will break loose. There are only three copies and the one I had in my safe belonged to the President.

It even had his hand written notes on it with his initials next them... Good grief, Bill, if that ever shows up in public it will all be over for the President and his administration.

"It can't be that bad. You talk like the President of the United States has suddenly become the worst horse thief in the world."

"I'm afraid that's exactly how it's going to look if that report becomes public, but that's not the worst of it. If the wrong people get their hands on that report, it could cause a blood bath and maybe even a war..." Jack took another swig of sour mash and put his glass down on the desk, with shaking hands.

"My God, Bill! They'll kill us all," he said.

CHAPTER SIX

JACK WAS IN GOOD condition for a man of his age but this situation was more than he could handle.

"You asked me to help you," I said. "If the situation is as bad as you say, it might involve the children, so tell me what's in that report."

"Okay, it's like this. Things have changed between the drug lords and the government in Bogotá. The cartels agreed to stop their war on the government in return for an end to extradition to the U.S., but they're blackmailing the government of Columbia in other ways. They've taken control of the finances of the country including the banks, the national treasury and most of the brokerage houses. They've intimidated or assassinated the reluctant heads of banks and any politicians who got in the way."

"It's part of a plan hatched by the drug interests throughout the world. The Columbians are taking control in Latin America, the Sicilians are moving into Europe, and the Chinese Tongs from Hong Kong are expanding their markets and control in the Pacific. They all need to launder large amounts of cash. They can't afford to tie up their assets in small amounts with slow, roundabout transfers. So, they're taking over international banks to launder their money."

"But the international banking laws control all that. There are agencies, people watching so it doesn't get out of control," I said.

"Yes and no. We got Noriega but the Columbian connection is

too strong. The same is true of Sicily and Hong Kong, but we nailed the International Bank of Commercial Credit and closed it down, freezing its assets in England and Belgium. That was a big one and it gave us the names of all the banks, the accounts, and conduits being used throughout the world by the major drug lords.

"Good, you have them on the run. So, what's the problem?"

He looked frantic. "Bill, the problem is we're part of a threatened species. The United States is a sitting duck and all the predators are closing in on us. Let me explain it this way. An economist is walking across the street, gets hit by a car, and ends up unconscious in a hospital. After twenty years in a coma, he wakes up and the first thing he asks is, 'what's the unemployment rate?' The answer comes back, 'zero'. He asks, 'what's the rate of inflation?' The answer is, 'zero'. 'Good grief,' he says. 'How much is a cup of coffee?' The answer comes back, 'ten yen'." We both got a laugh at that one.

"So we have a balance of payments problem. You can't buy a pair of shoes or a shirt made in the U.S. of A. any more but it works both ways. We buy their oil, televisions, and cars and they buy our wheat, guns, and airplanes so what's the point, Jack?"

"But don't you see? We have to keep the vultures away. We've tested it out and it works. Hong Kong is the heart of the heroin trade. The Chinese Tongs control that trade. Pick any day of the year and they transfer millions of dollars between major international banks. Think about it. What would happen if you could short circuit those transactions and put the money to good use on the world's financial markets? We did it to the International Bank of Commercial Credit and we bankrupted the bastards. Bill, we actually bankrupted the criminals. We took their money, twenty billion dollars, and we got away with it. That report in the safe, the one that was stolen tonight, was a detailed analysis of how we did it and a plan for doing the same thing to every drug cartel and international thief and robber we can identify. Until tonight, they didn't know who did it. If that report gets out, they'll know who took their money and how it was done."

"And they'll come after you with a vengeance...I'm sorry, Jack, but I don't buy it. You're not a rank amateur. You can't tell me you went out and stole twenty billion dollars from the drug cartels without realizing the risks. There has to be more."

"I never could fool you, Billy. A lot of powerful people are involved here and there's more at stake than I can begin to tell you."

"So, try me, Jack! Tell me what's really going on? When you get your hands on this money, what will you do with it?"

"Okay, it all begins when this country started the deregulation of the economy, banks in particular, but the problem is, other countries don't play by the same rules. It takes time and everything has to go through the legislative process and then we have to implement it."

"So, doesn't everyone have that problem? Why are we so unique?"

"Other countries: third world countries, the oil producers, all those other guys, they play by their own rules. They are not democracies. Our major banks made loans to third world countries and never got repaid. We financed real estate and business ventures in foreign countries and got skinned like we were country bumpkins coming to the big city for the first time. Some of our biggest banks are on the ropes. Bill! Damn it! Don't you see it? We're in danger of being taken over if we don't protect ourselves."

"So do we protect ourselves by becoming robbers and thieves?"

"The Senate Banking Committee is proposing legislation that will open up the industry even further. All major banking regulations date back to the New Deal legislation of the Roosevelt years and the Glass-Stegall act of 1934, which prevents bank mergers as well as other financial arrangements that led to the 1929 stock market crash."

"I've read about all that. It's nothing new and everyone has been talking about it for years," I said. "Why is this suddenly so important? We were the strongest country in the world. Now you tell me that we're being taken over by the Arabs, the Columbians, and the Chinese. It doesn't make sense"

"The new legislation will allow major investment banks, like the New York Trust and Commerce Bank, to merge with regional and branch commercial banks. In a few years there will be only about ten major banks and they'll own all the regional banks. These major 'Money Center' banks will need a lot of cash, and if they don't have it, the foreign investors will move in and buy up everything. It's a matter of liquidity. It's a horse race and our horses are old and tired. Theirs are young and fresh. They use drug money to win while we sit here playing by the rules."

"So you're going to use their drug money to bolster up our banks?"

"Yes, it's all worked out. No one will know where the money came from."

"I don't believe it. How are you going to launder the money?"

"Things are different now," Jack continued. "Today's big business executive knows no national loyalty. He reaps excessive profits by making his shirts in Sri Lanka for a dollar and selling them here for twenty-five dollars even if it puts American workers out of jobs. American oil companies manipulate the price of Arabian crude. They could care less if it hurts the American consumer and puts money into the pockets of third world dictators who subjugate innocent people and wage war on their neighbors. There are no patriots left." He slugged his drink down, with shaking hands.

"You've always been a patriot, Jack, but you never got involved in any dirty schemes and this is definitely dirty."

"You don't know how close we are to extinction. In 1997 the British left Hong Kong. The Chinese Tongs began to transfer their operations to San Francisco to avoid the Chinese government, which doesn't tolerate drug trafficking. They'll pollute this country with their heroin and dirty money. I'm retired, Billy. I'll never have another opportunity like this again. We need a strong, centralized banking system to fend off the foreign intruders and protect our domestic interests. Other countries do it, so why can't we?"

This was not like Jack. He was acting out of desperation and something had to be very wrong.

"Jack, who else is in on this with you?"

"I can't tell you everyone's name but we have representatives in every major bank. Salvatore Santiago is from the World Bank and Ambassador Kitterage is from the United Nations. Senator Cantrelli is on the Senate Foreign Relations Committee. Admiral James Rassmussen, Chief of Navy Procurement is our intelligence chief and I'm the director."

"How many meetings have you had with these people?"

"Only one, actually. The gathering tonight was supposed to be our operating committee meeting. Everyone was going to be here."

"All except Victor Cantrelli," I said.

"Yes, Victor went to the hospital with his body guard. He's family, you know, and he isn't expected to make it. It's really sad."

"It's an old shakedown trick. It keeps the rest of the victims in line while the pickers take what they can find."

"I don't know about that but did you have to kick that man in the face, Bill? I mean, look, I'm not criticizing you. I'm sure you used your best judgment but what if you hadn't resisted? What if you just let it pass and bought another locket for Samantha?"

"He grabbed Samantha and I can't replace her. Didn't you see that? I didn't want a shoot-out but they might have started shooting anyway. I took out the ones I could and as you saw, no one else got hurt."

"I can't say what I might have done if I were in your position. Natalie insists you caused the whole thing. I don't know what to do about her." He shook his head and stared off into space.

"Don't worry about it, Jack. She needs someone to blame, so I'm it. Just be thankful she isn't taking it out on you."

"The children are what worry me," he said. "I guess I'm feeling guilty because I spent so little time with the family when I was younger. I thought the money made up for it but I was wrong. It's ironic, is it not?"

"What is that, Jack?"

"I'm probably one of the most successful players in the international financial scene today. I've made decisions involving billions of dollars and millions of lives. I've made countries and I've broken them, and I did it without even stopping to catch my breath, but when it comes to my own family I'm totally helpless. That's why I admire you, Bill. You didn't hesitate to act tonight. Of all those men out there, you were the only one ready to face those robbers and protect your family."

"I did what I had to. Now, I have to know if you want me to help." The sound of a jet circling overhead filled the air.

"I need your help. We have an internal leak and I want you to find it. You'll be paid. I want you to watch everyone. There is no telling who it is. This program is important to the President and much of his support comes from the banking community."

"I usually work alone, but I will make an exception for you. Also,

I think you may need a bodyguard."

"The FBI will take care of that but I think you're right. We can't be too careful."

Jack looked out the jalousie windows behind his desk at the flashing red and green navigation lights of the approaching jet. We went out on the front patio where paramedics were loading bodies on stretchers and the local police were taking statements. It was a mess with tables, chairs, flowerpots, and broken glasses strewn everywhere. Connie came strolling over to me.

"Natalie took the children upstairs to bed. She didn't want them to see all this. I have to agree, they seemed overwhelmed."

"I'm overwhelmed myself," said Jack. "Why don't you two go inside and relax? I'll go up the hill to meet the FBI team, if you folks will excuse me. It looks like it's going to be a long night."

He walked away and I led Connie inside to the solarium in the north wing. We had the whole place to ourselves with an unlimited view of the countryside.

"William Thackery O'Keefe," she said. "I can't thank you enough for this bang up Fourth of July picnic. I just don't know when I've had so much fun and excitement. I'll have to put this in my book of days and nights to remember."

"What can I say, fair lady? When you rub elbows with the upper crust there's never a dull moment. Of course, one must occasionally liven things up by staging a robbery and shootout for the guests. That's why I always carry some heat, as they say." I pulled my Glock from its ankle holster, ejected the empty clip and re-holstered it.

"I didn't know you were carrying a gun," said Connie. "I'm not certain it makes me feel any safer. Judith and Natalie think you caused this whole disaster by resisting those thugs."

"People think carrying a handgun makes them safe but that's not always the case. The decision to pull out a loaded gun and fire it at someone is a show stopping decision. It changes the way you think and act for the rest of your life.

"Frankly, I could never understand how one human being could ever kill another. I was always taught the best way to avoid violence was not to resist," she said.

"That only works with reasonable, civilized people. Those waiters were cheap hoods. The one who grabbed Samantha was crazy. He really believed in his own immortality. I knew he was going to pull the trigger. A pro would have passed up the chance to get salted, but a punk can't let anything challenge his ego."

"So, you're saying you didn't cause any of it? That if you had just sat there he would still have tried something?"

"If he had walked by and not touched any of the kids, I wouldn't have done anything. Then there's the brotherhood thing."

"The what?"

"The brotherhood. You recognize it in the other fellow. If he's been blooded, that is to say if he has been under fire, you can tell by looking at him. He's part of the brotherhood and he has nothing to prove. That hood wanted to prove himself, and it was a mistake. When you encounter a man from the brotherhood, you don't test him out unless you're willing to fight for your life, and die."

"And what about you, Bill? Were you willing to fight and die then and there when he stuck that gun in your belly?"

"I made that decision before I stood up, and before I came here today. It was a decision I made years ago in Viet Nam, and when I came home from that war I made myself a promise that I would never step aside for anyone, ever again. I don't hunt trouble but it's there and I've learned to resist evil whenever I encounter it."

"What do you think your children learned tonight?"

"I hope they learned self respect. Being robbed is humiliating. Natalie and Judith take a superior attitude about such things, but those kids will eventually make their own decisions. They saw their father stand up to those thugs and in the long run they'll be proud. They also will learn who they can depend on when there is real trouble."

"I hope so, Bill, I sincerely hope so. I think Timothy was badly shaken by what he saw and I don't think he's all right."

"He will be, and when it comes time for him to make his decisions about life and the future, he'll be better informed than other kids his age. Don't worry, I am not finished with Timothy."

We settled in on the couch and held each other for a while, finding comfort in the closeness. Occasionally, a police car or ambulance would pass the windows overlooking the driveway, lights flashing, the siren cutting the darkness down the mountain. The view out the windows was still spectacular and before long I began to relax. I kept telling myself that everything was going to be all right. The problem was the shaking, always the damn shaking and the nausea. I knew it would go away, eventually. It always went away, I just had to hang on and it would go away. Connie put her arms around me and held me tightly.

"It's all right, Tiger. It's going to be all right," she said and I was glad we were alone.

CHAPTER SEVEN

I CAME OUT OF A deep snooze to find strangers standing over me. I had one of them by the throat and another one was trying to pull me away. Connie was sitting next to me, straightening herself up and wiping the sleep from her eyes. I let go of the man's Adams apple and he spoke with a hoarse voice.

"Sorry to bother you, sir." The man standing over me rubbing his neck was young, well dressed in a dark blue suit, medium build with short dark hair. A diamond stickpin held his tie in place.

"I'm FBI Agent Henry Corsini," he gasped, "and this is agent Joe Thomas." He referred to a man standing behind him.

Thomas was big and blond, wearing a light pink pastel jacket with a bulge on the left side and tight fitting tan pants. I relaxed my fist and sat up, trying to put it all together. It was still late and the moon was shining through the solarium glass above. I stretched and yawned, trying to orient myself.

"Sorry Mr., ahh…I must have fallen asleep."

"Corsini, sir and you are Mr. William Thackery O'Keefe?" He flashed his I.D. "Sorry if I startled you. Mrs. Sullivan said you were here and offered to come find you."

"You should have listened to her and you also should be very careful who you sneak up on."

"He said he was sorry, Mac." Blondie stepped in front of me in a threatening manner. "We do our job and we expect cooperation from you." Muscle, I love it.

"Back off, friend. I've already had my exercise tonight and I don't have anything to prove, OKAY?"

"It's all right, Mr. O'Keefe." Agent Corsini stepped in. "You're right, I should never sneak up on a man with your reputation. Look, can we talk?" He sat down across from the couch and pointed to a chair for his partner, Mr. Muscles. "Sit there, Joe." Joe reluctantly moved to the chair and sat down, but he never took his eyes off me.

"Mr. O'Keefe, it appears that you are a professional of some sort so maybe you can tell us what happened. We'll try to identify the waiter you injured and hope he lives so we can interrogate him, but we have very little to go on. These terrorist cases are usually a dead end requiring years to solve. We'll probably lose them in Montreal or Miami but we'll give it a try." He opened his notebook. "Now, what can you tell us about the terrorists?"

"They weren't terrorists," I said.

"What? What do you mean? They had to be terrorists. They fit the profile."

"That's what they want us to think but they weren't terrorists. They were punks; just cheap hoods. Terrorists don't steal jewelry and watches, they take hostages. They don't blow safes, they blow up buildings and pile up body counts in order to make political statements," I explained.

"But what about the AK-47s, the helicopters, the foreign clothes and accents? If they were just robbers, as you say, why would they go to all that trouble just for a few pieces of cheap jewelry? We came all the way from Washington with a special forensics team. We're from the Terrorist and Hostage Section of the FBI, so if they weren't foreign terrorists then we're wasting our time." He looked at me like I should be impressed.

"I didn't say they weren't foreigners. I said they weren't terrorists. There's a difference. These people were foreign but they were just hoodlums...gangsters."

"But how do you explain the organization, the weapons, and the helicopters?" asked agent Thomas.

"Look fellows, you said I was the only professional here who could help you. If you don't believe me, then why ask me all these questions? You can buy an AK-47 on any street corner in the Bronx. Helicopters and mercenaries are for sale everywhere. Hell, Corsini, if I'd known you were waiting for these guys in Montreal and Miami, I wouldn't have bothered going after them."

"We don't need your smart remarks, fella," said Agent Thomas. "We have more information on terrorism than you'll ever hope to see so just give us your cooperation and make things easy. We have a job to do and we're the professionals."

"Agent Thomas is right," said Corsini. "We're in charge of this investigation and we don't need civilians muddying up the waters. Just be available and don't talk about this to anyone else."

"Well don't let me keep you boys," I said standing up, "but just to set the record straight, this is my turf, my scene, my family, so don't be surprised if we cross paths again." I took Connie's hand and led her toward the door.

"Just one more question, if you don't mind," said Corsini. I turned and faced him. "What type weapon did you use to bring down that helicopter? Witnesses say it sounded like the Fourth of July up on that hill."

"Glock 17, used two full clips, and yes, it is the 4th of July."

"Geeze," said Thomas. "Nine millimeter parabellum. That's thirty four-slugs. Never could figure out the trigger mechanism on one of those. Must have been some show. Wish I'd seen it."

"I wouldn't know," I said. "I was concentrating on only one thing."

"Mind letting me see the gun?" asked Corsini. "We'll need it for our report."

"Next time you're in town, fellows," I said turning and I walked out with Connie by my side.

"What was that all about, Bill?"

"Not really sure but I won't risk any more friendly meetings with those people until I know what they're doing here. I'll wait to see what's going on before I give any more information to anyone, and that includes the FBI," I said as I led her out onto the patio.

"Does that include me too, Bill?"

"No, of course not. I'm sorry, Babe, things have really become crazy. What was supposed to be a family Fourth outing has turned into an international incident. It seems some of the guests here today were not just friends. They were here on business to discuss a highly classified report from the President of the United States regarding a plan to strengthen our domestic banking structure by stealing money from the international drug cartels."

"Oh no! Jack, your ex-father-in-law is involved in something like that?" exclaimed Connie.

"They already started using the plan by bankrupting the International Bank of Commercial Credit, an Arab owned institution that helped international terrorists, drug lords, arms dealers, and gangsters. The bank opened accounts for them, shuttled money around the world for their various activities, as well as just ordinary money laundering. Jack is one of the most respected men in international finance. Whoever blew that safe and stole that report is going to cause him a lot of trouble."

"This is incredible. Why did Jack ever think he could get away with such a thing? How were they planning to do it?" she asked.

"I don't know. Jack says they have a way and it works, but if that report gets loose and the drug cartels find out who is behind it, they'll probably start killing everyone involved."

"That's terrible. How could a man of Jack Sullivan's standing become involved in such a sleazy scheme? I mean after all, this house and the airplane. Look at it, he's got it made."

"He does, so why did he risk everything for such a stupid trick? He gave me a patriotic speech about saving America but I don't buy it. Something else is wrong. He asked me to help but it looks to me like there's enough professional muscle around to handle any investigation that's needed."

"So, what's our next move, Tiger? Do we go out hunting the quarry or do we wait for him to come to us?"

"I just don't know, Babe. This is not my sort of case. I'm an insurance investigator. This is an international case involving gangsters, dope dealers, banks, politicians, and murderers. Those aren't the kind of odds I'm prepared to tackle. I encountered all those things in Viet Nam and I don't intend to go back there again."

"So, pussy cat, are you saying that we're not getting involved in this one, no matter what?" She seemed disappointed.

"I think that pretty much sums it up. I don't enjoy seeing cheap punks grabbing at my daughter and I don't think she should be exposed to any more of that. The best way to prevent that is to stay out of this case and stay close to home. If they come after me again, then I'll get involved and there won't be any turning back until it's all over."

The patio was deserted and the moon had risen higher in the night sky. The flashing lights and sirens were gone with the bodies. The blood was still there and the familiar taped outlines showed where the bodies had been. There was a chill in the air. The wind had shifted to the northeast and a fog was forming in the valley. My thoughts turned to bed and curling up alongside Connie for the rest of the night, a not unpleasant prospect. My luck with women had not been all that great. That changed when I met Connie. She was a farm girl from Iowa and healthy was her middle name. I met her the year before on a case down on Long Island where she saved my life. She really knew how to treat a man. We had a good relationship and she got along well with the children. The day had been a success from that standpoint.

I looked out over the Hudson River valley and marveled at the brilliance of the star studded sky. I reflected on how we humans are nothing but miniscule specks in the greater scheme of the universe. What happened at the Sullivan's July 4th party was earthshaking in everyone's mind, but in the greater scheme of things it was nothing. My reveries were rudely interrupted by the arrival of my ex-wife and her mother.

"William! I have to talk to you," Natalie snapped as she approached. The look on Judith's face as she stood behind her daughter was too smug and determined. It was late and this was the last thing I needed.

"Mother and I have just gone through the absolutely horrible ordeal of putting the children to bed. They are so hyper, heaven only knows if they will ever sleep with all this violence and those FBI people guarding the place and flying overhead in their jet airplanes. I'll probably have to take a double dose of Valium just to get any rest tonight after what you've done. Why do you always resort to violence to solve every problem? I wish that man had killed you. Then we would all have some peace and quiet. We just can't continue living like this...," sob, "never," sob..."knowing when you're going to erupt again…," sob…"and ruin everything," sob, sob and sob.

Tears poured down her cheeks and her lower lip trembled as she talked. Any response to her hysteria at this point would invite a volcanic reaction lasting for hours. I wasn't about to give up the rest of my night to that sort of tyrannical behavior. I gave it my best shot while I was married to the woman, but nothing ever satisfied her, and now I was the object of all her unhappiness. That's what divorce is all about you know. You don't have to put up with it any more. So, I made a decision to put a stop to it.

"Tell you what, Natalie, since I'm such a bad person, you probably don't want me to stick around so I'll leave. We'll find a room for the night at a motel and then you won't have to worry about me destroying your life. Of course you won't have me to blame for everything either, so good night and good luck." I took Connie by the arm and gently guided her toward the door.

"That's not fair!" Judith said, deciding to join the fray. "Natalie is only expressing her feelings and frankly I am inclined to agree. We are not accustomed to having our parties end in bloodshed, and you of all people should know that."

"Judith, you should be very careful about choosing sides in this battle. You and Jack are in no position to suddenly become picky about who you let play on your team. Those thugs may come back and all your charm and money won't protect you. Just think about one thing. Remember that those children are upstairs in bed right now and not on one of the helicopters being taken as hostages.

The only thing standing between you and those killers is one man and that's me, Baby. I'm one man who doesn't give a damn about your social status or your garden parties, one man who will fight to the death to protect his family. Think about that and think carefully about what's important to you, and then take your daughter to a shrink and get her oil and water checked, because she's got her wires crossed and she's short circuited." I turned and started to leave.

"Wait, Bill, please," Judith pleaded. "I...I am sorry...don't go, please...I have to talk to you." I turned to find her crying. I'd never seen Judith shed a tear. She was always too tough and competent. I turned back and Connie followed.

"Mother!" cried Natalie. "Don't give into this animal. He'll ruin everything. I won't have it, I absolutely won't have it!" She stamped her foot and clenched her fists. The veins in her neck and forehead stood out. I'd seen this act many times and evidently so had Judith.

"Natalie! Go to the kitchen and make us some coffee. It's going to be a long night." Judith still had amazing control. Natalie made to object but Judith gave her a stern fixed stare.

"I'll go with you, if it's all right," said Connie. She took Natalie by the arm and led her away, leaving me with Judith. I've never been comfortable when women from my past get together on a friendly basis, but Connie was a levelheaded gal.

"After all," I mumbled to the wind, "what else can go wrong?" Little did I know.

CHAPTER EIGHT

JUDITH HAD REGAINED HER composure. "William, come and sit down, please. I have to say, first of all, that I agree with you. I just cannot tolerate the manner in which you say it, but I have no choice. Jack is in very serious trouble. Actually, he has gotten us into an impossible pickle and I don't know what to do about it. I'd make a contract with the devil right now if I thought it would help, but since the devil isn't present, I must deal with you." She seemed to slur her words; very unusual for Judith. I thought she might just be tired.

"I'm flattered," I said. At least I thought I was.

Jack and Judith Sullivan were very rich. They could hire anyone and that went all the way to the White House. Instead, they were turning to me. I was flattered but was I being a fool?

"Jack tells me you offered to protect him. That's very generous but I'm afraid it's not enough. He won't tell anyone what's going on. I am so angry that he got involved with these people that I could just strangle him." She stopped and sniffed, her bottom lip quivering.

"I don't buy the patriotic story about saving American banks. Why did he get involved in such a mess?" I asked. I noticed her eyes were slightly glazed over.

"I don't understand it myself," she said." There are times when I think Jack is naive about the real world. He has helped so many people and never received anything in return for his efforts and now he's in this mess and no one will help him."

"Money doesn't solve all our problems, Judith. It just attracts a lot of greedy, shallow, fair weather friends. It's like honey, when it's all gone, the flies leave and the party's over. Money buys attention and excitement, but not friends."

"You have such a graphic way of describing things, William. I think Natalie is right. You are such an animal, yes, but then we are living in a jungle, are we not, and what we need is an expert in jungle warfare and you are it. The thing I like about you is your will to win at any cost. No wonder Natalie was no match for you." She lit a cigarette with shaking hands and gave it a couple of unladylike puffs. "So tell me, William, is there anything at all in life that scares you?"

"Yes, what scares me most is that you and Natalie will stop hating me and I'll have to be nice to you the rest of my life."

"Lord preserve us, William, you are some piece of work. I will tell you something. Frankly, I was glad when Natalie divorced you but then she started coming home more often... (puff, puff)...here... (puff, puff)...and I got the feeling of what a shrew she has become...(puff). I thought at first you really had done all those terrible things and then she turned on me. She accused me of doing the most awful things to her when she was young. That's when I realized how unstable she had become, and I started to understand what you had gone through. I don't know what to do now. I am deathly afraid to disagree with her because she becomes so vicious and at times...well...violent." She shook her head and stretched.

"Have you tried a psychiatrist?"

"Oh, heavens, yes! There was a Dr. Goldman down in Scarsdale where we lived when she was young. That was a terrible disaster. He became totally convinced she was all right and we were all crazy. He was completely taken by her. So, we transferred her to a Dr. Habib in Valhalla and the same thing happened. After six months he declared himself to be in love with her and he could not treat her any longer. At that point we didn't know what to do, so we just stood back and hoped for the best."

"Has she improved at all?" I asked.

"When the slightest little thing goes wrong, she explodes and goes into one of her tirades blaming you for everything. We have no experience in handling this sort of anger."

She was right about that. They lived in a world where it was considered a weakness to display overt anger. Everything was handled by pretending there were no problems. That was because rich people don't have problems.

"There may be a reason for her behavior," I offered.

"What's that? Is there something I don't know?" She took a drag on her cigarette and tried to flick the ashes but missed the cigarette instead.

"Jack said he was not around much when Natalie was growing up. She was raised mostly within the confines of private girls' schools and she's had very bad luck with men."

"You can say that again," she said, trying to find her mouth with the cigarette. It was then I realized she was slightly tipsy.

"Okay, I will, her experience with men has been limited and not very successful. I think she's angry and resentful about that, and she blames Jack for not being there as a father."

"But she never has said that," puff, puff.

"It's not safe to become angry with people you love. They might leave you and never come back. So she takes it out on me because I'm not around and that's safer."

"But what about the way she treats me?"

"There's a strong bond between mother and daughter. She knows you won't leave her. Her attacks on me were safe because she knew I'd never abuse her or the children. I might shoot a criminal for trying to abduct my daughter, but I would never hurt Samantha or strike her mother. Natalie knows me better than you think. She's more afraid of being abandoned than she is of violence."

"I have to tell Jack about this. So, what do you advise?"

"Simple, Judith, lots of hugs and kisses. What they call warm fuzzies. Let your hair down and show some emotion. It's easier with the children so start there. It's called love and you don't need money to do it."

"You don't pull your punches do you, Mr. O'Keefe."

"I grew up in a small upstate farming community where values were different from the world of big money and influence."

"I don't need your scorn, William," she puffed as she talked.

"I said different, that's all. You can make judgments at another time and place, okay? So, TRUCE!" I raised my hand.

"Fair enough. I will try and so will Jack, I promise." Natalie and Connie came out carrying trays with cups, coffee and cookies.

"We'll have to talk again about all this, William," and that was the end of the conversation as she stubbed out her cigarette.

"We have coffee, tea, and cookies," Natalie chirped. She was more animated than I'd seen her in years. "Connie showed me a trick in making coffee. Bet you can't guess what it is."

"We'll give it a try," I said, winking at Judith. "Right now, anything hot, wet, and strong, is welcome."

"Oh, there you go again, William, with the innuendo. You are an animal and Connie agrees with me." She giggled.

We chatted and swigged hot steaming coffee, chewed on dark brown oatmeal cookies, and watched the stars. It was well after midnight and a chill wind was wafting down the mountain. I noticed high wispy cirrus clouds moving in from the west across the pale green moon. Jack appeared at the door and peered out at us.

"Come and have some coffee, dear." Judith was ever the proper hostess.

"Man! Those FBI guys never give up. They must have asked me the same questions a hundred times, over and over again. I don't understand what they're looking for," he said.

"Neither do they," I said. "They're just muddying up the waters."

"What do you mean?" Jack looked perplexed as he sat down.

"What I mean, Jack, is that maybe you're expendable. Maybe these FBI drones are here just to cover up what's happened."

"You really don't mean that, do you?" Judith stared at me. "Whatever makes you say that, William?"

"Their attitude, their procedures, their lack of questions for starters. Let me put it this way, folks. How long did they spend talking to you, asking you questions?"

"They haven't asked me anything," Judith replied.

"They ignored me completely," said Connie.

"The big handsome one with the muscles asked where the bathroom was," Natalie giggled as she nibbled a cookie.

"So, they didn't interview Natalie, Connie, Judith, the children,

the cook, the maid, the gardener, or any of the guests, right?"
"What is this, William," asked Judith, "An interrogation?"

"Yeah, more questions, but not the kind the FBI is asking, or rather, isn't asking."

"I see what you mean," said Jack, "but why would they do that?"

"I'm not sure but they don't seem to care if they catch those waiters or the ones behind it all."

"So, why are they here?" asked Connie.

"Probably to make certain Jack is not at the bottom of it all and to cover up the whole incident. I've seen this before. Standard procedure requires an on-the-spot interview of all available witnesses as soon after the crime as possible. No one is ever overlooked. These yo yo's are not your normal FBI investigators. They're just a bunch of janitors, a clean up crew sent here to scrub the decks and make it all pretty again.

Jack was very quiet, looking down at his feet. Judith stared at me with a look that said, "Knock it off". Natalie just kept on chattering to no one in particular like nothing was going on, and Connie sipped her coffee intently as if it were a gourmet delight. My speech had not fallen on deaf ears but it was late and everyone was tired. Tomorrow would be another day so I decided to let it go but then Jack persisted.

"Well, this doesn't make any sense," he said, breaking the silence. "I suppose I'll have to go to Washington and explain all this when these FBI people are done but I should consult with some of the others involved in tonight's planning session."

"Haven't you done enough?" asked Judith. "I mean, really dear, you are retired and we have more than enough to live on comfortably so why do you have to continue working like this?" Jack looked at me with a helpless expression on his face.

"It's hard to turn down a request to work with the top people in the government," I said. "I guess I would do the same as Jack if I got a call from the White House."

"Is that true?" Judith asked, looking at Jack with surprise. "Are you doing this for the President?"

"Yes, well, sort of," he said. "I was going to tell you all about it but Bill has let the cat out of the bag. I really can't say too much about it.

It's Top Secret you know?"

Just as I was thinking of how to disengage from the shocked silence that followed, there was a commotion in the house and the children came boiling out of the main doors ahead of a frantic agent Joe Thomas. Little Jonathan led the charge followed by Samantha and Timothy. Thomas appeared somewhat disoriented.

"Sorry...ahh...folks," Agent Thomas said, breathing hard. "They slipped right by me. Didn't have a chance...they were on me before I knew it."

"We wanted to say goodnight to everyone," Jonathan blurted out throwing his arms around Jack's neck.

"Goodnight, Grandma," Samantha gave Judith a hug and a kiss.

Timothy stood next to Connie with his hand laid tentatively on her shoulder. It was a free-for-all as everyone was getting mauled with hugs and kisses. Natalie, always fearing intimacy, made the first move to break it up.

"Now, you have all broken the rules and I will decide on your punishment tomorrow morning." That'll give them something to sleep on, I thought. "Right now it is time to go back to sleep." She continued. She stood and pointed toward the house and yelled, "Move!"

I turned and found Timothy standing next to me, a look of blank despair on his face, his hand on the back of my chair. I stood up, grabbed Jonathan under the left armpit and swung him up over my head so that he landed astride my shoulders, facing forward. We'd done this act so many times it was second nature and he never failed to help by swinging his legs up and over my head so he landed safely on my shoulders, legs around my neck. I put out my right hand for Samantha and my left for Timothy who grabbed hold so hard he dug his fingernails into the flesh of my left palm. I gave him a wink and he lightened his grip.

"Folks, this is a family day so all of you will please follow me."

I headed for the house with everyone trailing behind me. I was the pied piper leading his lost army home, followed of course by the FBI.

CHAPTER NINE

"IF YOU WAKE UP in the morning and count your toes, how many should you have on each foot?"

That was how Sergeant Harry Gramanski started his combat orientation program when I arrived in Viet Nam. We all thought he was kidding. However, it seems there was a young lieutenant that Gramanski served under for a short while at a fire base in the midlands. The lieutenant liked a good night's sleep so he always left the night duty to his Sergeant. One morning the lieutenant woke up and noticed he had no shoes or socks on his feet. He also noticed his right foot had six toes and his left had four. He thought about it for a while and decided everything was all right because he still had a total of ten toes.

What he didn't know was that during the night there was an attack and his right leg was blown off by a mortar shell in the first barrage. That same shell blew off his left big toe. The medics placed a tourniquet on his right leg, took off his left boot, swabbed the stump of the big toe and gave him an extra big shot of morphine until they could med-evac him out to a field hospital. So, what about the other foot with six toes? It seems this NVA regular came over the wire, got blown away and landed in the foxhole next to the lieutenant. He had no shoes but he did have six toes on one foot and that was the foot next to the lieutenant's. A six toed gook?

"Yeah," said Sergeant Gramanski, "the gook had six toes on one foot."

"So, what's the moral of the story?" we asked.

"Simple," said the good sergeant. "When you wake up, count your toes and make sure you have the right number of body parts and confirm that they're in the right place."

"What are you doing, William Thackery O'Keefe?" Connie asked.

"Counting my body parts."

"What? You're what?" She sat up in bed.

"Counting my toes."

"Do I have to ask why, or should I just skip it?"

"You can always ask."

Judith invited us to stay upstairs in one of the guest bedrooms of the main house after putting the children back to bed, so I had to retract my threat of going to a motel. We slept late and the sun was shining brightly over the hill into our windows.

"I won't ask next time I see you doing something strange. I can't take any more of these Viet Nam stories," Connie said.

"It's part of my history and it won't go away. That's what happens when they make you into something for which there is no peacetime equivalent. They taught us to breathe through our ears. Then they sent us home and we weren't allowed to breathe through our ears any more, so there we were, all ears and no place to go. Sometimes I forget and start breathing through my ears again and everyone gets up and moves to the back of the bus."

"You talk a lot in metaphors."

"It's less painful that way. I don't have to let people get too close. There's always a metaphor between us."

"So, how close can I get, Mr. O'Keefe?"

"As close as you like, but if you're a moth, beware of the flame."

"Another metaphor." She rolled into me. "Is this too close?"

She did some naughty things and before long we were in the throes of passionate lovemaking. I marveled at the beauty and perfection of this lady's body, the firmness of her breasts and her soft smooth skin. This was a woman I could lose myself in time and again and still come back for more as if it were the first time. She was always there to take care of me, something I was not accustomed to, yet I had no complaints. After our loving, we held each other and I was headed for sleep again when there was a knock at the door.

"Yes? Who's there?" I called out, trying to wake up.

The door opened and Jonathan's small face appeared in the crack, his eyes closed and a large grin on his face.

"Grandma says it's time for breakfast. She said not to look, all right?"

"Yes, okay, we'll be right there. Don't eat all the pancakes before I get there, Jonnie. I'm as hungry as a horse at haying time."

"Okay, Dad," he said, "and can I look now?"

"Sure." He opened his eyes and looked at us buried under the covers. "You're not doing anything. Mother said to keep my eyes closed and not to look in case you were doing something."

"Go tell your mother we're not doing anything and to save me some pancakes. Now get!"

I winked and threw my pillow at him. He slammed the door and ran. I could hear his stocking feet and the giggles of the other kids behind him as they ran along the hallway and down the stairs.

"You fit into this domestic scene very well, Bill. After seeing you in action last night, I sometimes wonder if you'll ever settle down to the quiet life of home and family."

"Good point. I was really adrift after the divorce. The judge took everything except my sailboat and Granddad's summer cottage in the dunes. If Natalie had her way, she would have taken those too just out of spite. They took my house, my tools, my desk and chair, even the bureau where I kept my clean underwear. Many men never overcome that sort of shock to the system."

"You've overcome it and you seem contented now," Connie said.

"Living alone on Long Island was about the safest thing I could do. Staying away from people suited me. I still had Willie Monk as a friend and partner. He was a tough old bird and he understood me. Now, you're in my life and we're here in the great house playing at a form of domestic bliss that scares the hell out of me. Not that I'm afraid of involvement with you or responsibility for the kids. It's just... well...like last night, I'm no ordinary father. I'm not even your usual, ordinary, run-of-the-mill insurance investigator. When someone shows up with an AK-47, instead of acting terrified and totally cowed, I stare the joker in the eye and dare him to pull the trigger. That's called breathing through your ears and it tends to cause a lot of trouble." I watched as Connie got out of bed.

"So, you're afraid the next challenge may be your last, is that it?" She said as she began brushing her hair.

"If I were the only one, there would be no problem. I worry for everyone around me. Natalie was right in a way about last night, but she's wrong about how it happened. They said I caused the incident last night because I'm a violent person. That's not true. It's just that violent things happen around me because of the circumstances and the people with whom I deal."

"So, you're saying that you can't pass up a challenge and you're afraid innocent people will be hurt if they're near you."

"I guess that's about it. When it's just you and me, it's two consenting adults, but it's not the same when we add the kids. Timothy never asked for what he saw last night and he didn't deserve it. He would not have seen that dead pilot if I hadn't gone up that hill. He trusted me and he got more than a kid his age deserved for that trust."

"You're playing a different tune this morning. Is Tiger feeling guilty?"

"Yes, and I'm worried about what's going to happen in the near future. Those goons could come back any time. I don't think we should wait around to see what happens."

"I agree," said Connie, climbing out of bed, "but I doubt that Natalie will let the kids out of her sight. They're her security blanket. Last night I realized she uses them like a weapon to get her way. You should be careful what you agree to do with her."

"Are we just a wee bit jealous?" I said.

"Not in the least, buster." Connie turned and faced me, stark naked, feet spread, hands on her hips and said, "Does this look like jealousy? Because if you think that, you're living in la la land."

"Impressive!" I said. "Very impressive."

"Thank you," she said as she turned and strutted her stuff into the bathroom!

Breakfast was in the north wing solarium where Connie and I were the previous night. Maria, dressed in her starched, lace-fringed, gray cotton uniform poured our orange juice and coffee, took our orders, and rushed off to the kitchen. Everyone seemed subdued. Even the children, seated at another table in a far corner, were unusually quiet. When I was a kid, everyone sat around the table and participated in the family's conversations. That way a child grew up and learned right from wrong.

"We've been waiting for you to come down to discuss the day's plans." Judith was unusually severe. Natalie, pale and red eyed, sat stone-faced and silent.

"What do you have in mind?" I said trying to play it cool.

"What the hell do you think we have in mind, William?" Natalie snapped. "Do you think we all enjoy waiting for you while you and your girlfriend get it on upstairs?"

"Natalie, please! Not in front of the children. They have had a terrible time after last night," Judith snapped and then she continued.

"As you know, William, Jack and I always go to Pamplona the day after the Fourth of July for the running of the bulls and we've never missed a season. This will be the fortieth anniversary. We're scheduled on a flight out of Kennedy for Barcelona at 3:00 PM this afternoon. We have friends waiting for us in the Plaza del Castillo and seats reserved at the Cafe' Iruna at 5:00 PM tomorrow. I do not intend to miss it."

She finished with her eyes locked defiantly on mine. I knew all about this and had even gone with them on two occasions. They had a villa on the road north of town leading to Roncesvalles Pass going into France. Jack ran every morning with the bulls during the Fiesta at 7:00 A.M. He'd never been gored or trampled.

"Well, as they say folks, bon voyage," I said. "I'll be out of here as soon as breakfast is over and you can be on your way. Hope you have a nice trip." Connie agreed and we drank our orange juice. "Is that it?" Natalie blurted out. "That's all you have to say?" "If there's something you want from me, just ask and don't speak in riddles. There are more then enough mysteries in life." The orange juice suddenly tasted bitter. She had that effect on people.

"What she is trying to say, William, is...well, I suppose you must have it spelled out for you. Someone needs to watch over the children.

So the question we have for you is this, are you prepared to meet your obligations as a father by providing for their care or will it be necessary for us to make other arrangements?"

"Why don't you just take them along? They'd enjoy a few weeks in Spain and the whole trip would be highly educational," I said.

"Please, no, William. This is our time, just Jack and I. We have always done it that way." Judith sat erect and resolute.

I realized I was being punished and I had to pay my dues. I had brought Connie to a family gathering and that embarrassed Judith and Natalie, so now they would make me pay.

"Look, Judith," Jack said, "we can skip the bulls this year. It's no big deal. It's more important for us to be here right now."

"Don't be silly, Jack dear." Judith laid her hand on his arm and squeezed. "We always go to Pamplona for the Fiesta. Everyone will miss us. The servants will all be expecting us. What will we tell the newspapers? You're a legend, the only American to run with the bulls every year for forty years and besides, we can use a change. Things are out of hand around here," she turned to me, "and that's where you come in, William. We cannot go unless you take care of this whole mess. I just cannot leave with all these loose ends, William, and you will just have to step forward and take some responsibility. After all, William, you did have a hand in causing it." I liked her better when she was drunk.

"Okay, Judith! Go to Spain and take Jack with you. I'll take the kids to my place and Natalie can take some time off for herself."

"No! I don't want him to have the children. He's a violent, dangerous animal and he'll poison their minds!"

"Natalie, why don't you grow up?" Connie said. "You're an adult woman with three children to care for and all you do is complain. I'm a guest here so you'll probably never invite me back again, and I frankly don't care except for those poor kids. You use them as weapons to get your way and it's hurting them. Why don't you get with it, grow up and live a productive life?" Connie said as she cut a chunk of butter and slapped it on her English muffin.

The silence that followed Connie's speech was so heavy you could hang your hat on it. She was probably right, we would never be invited back so I decided to try something creative.

"I have an idea. Why not ask the kids what they want to do?"

"What do they know?" Natalie sneered.

"Shut up!" Judith said. "Shut up and let the rest of us solve this problem!" Natalie opened her mouth but shut it again.

Judith said, "I suppose if we are to solve this problem we will have to let you do it your way, William, so proceed," and I did.

Timothy and Jonathan opted for a sailing vacation with me while Samantha chose her mother's company after several warning looks from Natalie. Later I would look back on this moment and wonder what might have happened if I had not been so darned creative.

CHAPTER TEN

IT TOOK TIME TO sort out everyone's luggage and say our goodbyes. Samantha kept hanging around the car as we were loading up and I thought of taking her with us, but her mother would go off the deep end for sure. We were traveling in Connie's little Japanese compact and space was a problem, but we finally got everyone in place and we were ready to go. Then agent Corsini showed up just as we were about to leave.

"We have a few loose ends to wrap up before you go, Mr. O'Keefe. Could you join us in the office?"

The room was full when I arrived. Jack sat at his desk with Agent Corsini standing on his right and Agent Thomas on his left. Deputy Kim Woo stood by the bookcase to my left as I entered the room, and there were three other men sitting in chairs to the right. Judith was serving coffee and she gave me a sour look as I walked in. Jack made the introductions.

"Ah, Bill, have a seat. You know everyone here, I believe, except the forensics team. That's Mr. Smith, Mr. Marcusi, and Mr. Allen."

I nodded and they returned the nod. I nodded to Agent Corsini. He nodded back. I smiled at Jack. He smiled back. Agent Thomas glared at me so I glared at him. I looked at Deputy Woo. He looked back and shrugged, so that was it. Nobody knew anything and they were all waiting for me, so I sat down and tried to act disinterested.

"What's up, guys?" I said looking around.

"Before everyone leaves," Corsini began, "we want to take a look at what's happened and draw some conclusions so there are no misunderstandings down the road. I thought it would be easier now to share the information we have and then we can agree on some future course for the investigation. First of all, we have decided to treat this as a terrorist attack of a one-time nature. I've been on the phone to the Director and we don't believe they will be back, because they got what they came after. Also, the Sullivans are leaving for Spain and two of the children are going with Mr. O'Keefe, so the chances of the terrorists following any of them is very remote. Mrs. O'Keefe and one child will be staying here, so we will provide a minimum security net for one week on the estate itself just as a precaution. Agent Thomas and I will share that duty. We will go two shifts, twelve on and twelve off. Shouldn't be too tough, should it, Joe?" Joe nodded at Corsini and glared at me.

"Do you think two of you will be enough if those terrorists come back?" asked Jack.

"We're equipped and trained to handle terrorist attacks. We can deal with whatever comes," answered Agent Thomas.

"They'll be back and they'll come when you least expect it with more firepower than you can muster," I said.

"How do you know that, Mr. O'Keefe? Have you been in contact with them?" asked Corsini.

"I don't know anything more than you do, fellas, and that should be enough. They came the first time to steal something. The next time they come, it will be for revenge."

"You're just assuming that, Mr. O'Keefe. We're all grateful for what you did but we have to work on facts, not assumptions."

"Suit yourselves fellows. Me, I'm going sailing."

"We wish we had that option," said Corsini. "There are still some items of interest we need to go over. First, there is the helicopter which Mr. O'Keefe managed to bring down last night."

He passed out eight by ten glossies of the crashed aircraft. It had gone in on its left side in a small field, skidding into a stone wall and a line of mountain grown white oak trees. It was not a pretty sight. I'd seen many like it in Viet Nam and I never got used to the bodies sprawled helplessly around the wreckage.

The helicopter represented many things in that war. It offered mobility and tactical superiority in a war of attrition. To the Viet Cong it meant death and destruction. For the GI it represented transport to safety and salvation from the many traps the VC could set in the jungles. For some of us it was a two edged sword. The Huey was an effective fighting machine, but it was vulnerable to ground fire and more than one squad fought its way to the landing zone and a successful pickup only to end up being shot down. That's why they called them 'flying coffins'.

"We identified the aircraft as an Italian built Agusta, A109A with fully retractable landing gear. It has twin Allison 250 Turbo shaft engines, a cruise speed of 169 mph and a range of 345 miles. We are checking with the manufacturer in Italy to find out where this one was purchased and delivered. We're working on the bodies but none of them have been ID'd. They all wore the same outfits but none had any personal items. This was a well-organized, highly trained, para-military group and our chances of nailing them are very slim. We're even lucky to have the chopper and the terrorists it was carrying. So far we found six slugs from Mr. O'Keefe's weapon in the aircraft itself. One did hit the tail rotor and damaged a blade, which may account for the steep angle at which they went in. Another was found in the turbine itself and it caused a great deal of internal damage to the left engine."

The report went on, interspersed with the usual technical jargon and tempered by typical bureaucratic hedging, like: "The alleged attacker, who was rendered incapacitated by Mr. O'Keefe's apparent actions on behalf of his daughter, whom it has been alleged was touched by one of the terrorists..." etc and etc.

I was tempted to say something about the alleged gun the alleged SOB had in his alleged hand, but I didn't feel like arguing with alleged official ignorance. Finally, we came to the forensics team: fingerprints, blood samples, and dental evidence, clothing, explosives, and detonator fragments.

"We've examined the clothing and the only lead we have to follow up is the footwear," said Mr. Allen. All the attackers, including the pilot of the helicopter, were wearing alligator shoes and belts, dyed black. They were handmade custom fitted shoes with no label, but there is a mark inside of each shoe which appears to be the initials of the cobbler. We can't really make them out but we will in time." Agent Corsini handed one of the shoes around for everyone to examine and then he continued to talk.

"We're checking Miami on this one since Florida is probably the origin of most alligator hides, and that would tie into the terrorist connection..."

"Lizard!" said Deputy Kim Woo, looking at the shoe.

"What?" Corsini stopped short in his presentation.

"This isn't alligator," said Woo, "it's lizard, North African Mowangi lizard, similar to the Tex-Mex Chuckwalla lizard only with spines like the Tuatara. Looks a lot like a small alligator. The shoes are Italian made, very expensive, and much sought after. The mark you referred to, Mr. Allen, is not the cobbler's mark, it is a clan sign of either the Libyan or Moroccan tribe where this lizard skin was purchased."

"How do you know all this, Mister Woo?" asked Thomas. "We have the best forensics team in the world and no one came up with lizard. How come?"

"I was stationed at Terjon Air Force Base in Spain for three years. I used my time to study the area surrounding the Mediterranean. The Air Force carried these shoes in their commissary for a while, until the commander's wife and her afternoon tea club found out the lizards were considered an endangered species. Hell, you would never know it if you went to Morocco and rode a camel around the desert. The Mowangi lizards are everywhere. We used to call them the Moroccan Jack rabbit. They're little ugly green things about two feet long. The tribesmen use them for target practice. They try to shoot their eyes out while riding atop a running camel or horse."

"You got around a lot over there, Deputy. What was your classification?" asked Corsini.

"Intelligence. I had authorization to travel and a lot of free time. We were encouraged to travel through as many countries as possible to gather general intelligence information. I spent most of my time in Morocco, Algeria, Libya, and Ethiopia. I saw things you would never believe, like a Moroccan tribesman shooting a Mowangi lizard off a rock at a hundred yards from the back of a running horse with a muzzle-loading rifle."

"It's an interesting story, Deputy," said Thomas, "but our forensics team has determined these are alligator shoes so the issue is closed. I don't buy your story even as entertaining as it is. I don't believe anyone in his right mind would make shoes out of lizards."

"We are committed to an investigation of terrorists rooted in the Miami area and that's how we'll proceed," Corsini jumped in.

Woo looked at me and raised his eyebrows and I shrugged. It was obvious we weren't part of it. Bureaucracy always wins in the face of logic, so I decided to let well enough alone. Besides, I wasn't sure what I could do. The whole affair was out of my hands now. I just wanted it to be over so I could go sailing. The Fourth of July picnic was over, the fireworks were gone in a flash, and soon I would be also. The meeting was over and the forensics team packed it off in the Lear jet leaving Agents Corsini and Thomas behind to play guard dog.

I went to collect the kids and Connie for the ride home, but instead found Jack and Judith standing next to the car with Connie in the driver's seat, a look of consternation on her face.

"The children have changed their minds, William," said Judith. "They will be staying here with Natalie since the FBI has decided to provide protection. They will be safer this way and besides they need their mother."

My first impulse was to strangle the arrogant witch. I knew darned well that the boys would never pass up a chance to go sailing with me, but I also knew better than to challenge Judith because she never forgave anyone who questioned her veracity. It was better to work around her, go along with her snobbish deception, and find a way later on to spend time with the kids.

"I'll just go say goodbye to the children, if you don't mind," I said, making a move toward the house.

"No! Please don't, William. It would be better if you didn't upset them right now. They should remain with their mother and the last thing they need is to be reminded of last night's disaster." She stood erect and defiant, blocking my path to the house.

"All right, Judith," I said giving in, "but someday soon we will have to talk about this. I'll leave you with one last thought and I want you to consider it very carefully. If I was really as violent and unpredictable as you and your spineless daughter keep saying, you could well be dead right now for what you've just done. Meanwhile, you folks have a nice trip and watch out for all that BULL!" Judith spun around and stomped off in a rage and I turned to go. Jack looked at Judith with an expression of pained resignation and just shook his head while staring off into the distance.

"Wait, Bill, please wait a moment," he said, almost pleading. "I'd like a word with you before you leave." The tone of his voice and his troubled expression stopped me cold.

"Will this never end?" I thought, as I turned and faced him.

CHAPTER ELEVEN

I WAS NOT IN THE mood for a chat. All I wanted to do was get away from the fog of phoniness that surrounded the Sullivan estate. Yet Jack was a decent man and a friend so I owed him at least the courtesy of a fair hearing. The look of panic on his face stopped me in my tracks.

"All right, Jack. I've never told you what I really thought about this family and the way my children are being treated. I'll let it pass for now out of respect for you and our friendship but there have to be some changes made and soon, or those kids are going to end up so bent they won't be able to find their way to the toilet without a seeing eye dog!"

"I quite agree," he said. "I promise I'll help straighten this out when we come back. I've seen some things this weekend that I never realized were happening before. I guess I've just been ignoring them but there's something more important right now that we have to discuss."

"What could be more important?" I shot back.

"Bill, I didn't tell you everything before...I...I am sorry but this is very difficult for me. Please, can we take a walk?" He took my arm and guided me toward the tennis courts. "We'll be just a few minutes, Connie. Sorry for the delay." Connie nodded, took a book from her purse and started reading. I think it was one of those romance novels.

At least I hoped it was.

We walked in silence until we reached the tennis courts. Then Jack led the way up the hill to the airstrip, talking as we went.

"Last night you asked me why I've become involved in such a risky affair as this bank deal, and I owe you a better explanation. It's the money. You see, we're broke. I've lost almost all my money and the creditors are closing in on me."

"You got to be kidding, Jack. How did that happen?"

"I've been taken to the cleaners and there isn't enough left to keep this house and our lifestyle going. I've tried to keep up the pretense of wealth, but it won't be long and I'll lose it all," he said, staring at the ground.

"But how, Jack? The house must be paid for and you salted away millions in a diversified portfolio. I helped you set it up myself so I know what you're worth."

"No you don't. I changed things around and got snookered. I can't even believe it myself but I made a classic blunder. I put all my eggs in one basket, Executive Mutual of New Jersey. It's all gone."

"Oh no! Good grief, man, how could you? I explained that plan to you when I set it up. It was a standard annuity. You could get the same plan from any number of insurance companies but no plan is any better than the company that sells and underwrites it. Jersey Mutual is a moderate to high-risk company, remember? I said not to put more than a hundred grand into that plan."

"But it paid eight and three quarters, guaranteed, and when the market tanked, I decided to go into Jersey Mutual to make up my losses. I was desperate. Besides, I didn't have to pay taxes on my earnings until I spent them. I thought it would only be temporary, and then some of my real estate ventures went sour and I needed a safe place to hide everything until it all blew over and the economy picked up."

"But it didn't," I said.

"No it didn't, and then Jersey Mutual went under without any warning. I can't understand how that happened. It's like the money just disappeared, as if it was siphoned off. They said it was bad investments in junk bonds and the records are all lost because of computer failures, high staff turnover, and a fire in the main office.

It all sounds very fishy to me."

"Me too, Jack. How much did you have invested?"

"I'm embarrassed to say...it was everything...almost eighty-eight million. All my liquid assets and I put a mortgage on my house to keep it safe just in case."

"Oh no! How did you make the transfer of funds? You didn't just send them a check did you?" I stared at him in disbelief.

"Their Chief Executive Officer, Anthony Pinucci, handled it. There were no records kept so the money couldn't be traced. I had creditors chasing me on the real estate investments, so I didn't want a trail left behind. I was on the brink of bankruptcy. I was desperate."

"And Anthony was only too happy to help, right?" He nodded. "So is this the reason you got involved in that scheme to rob the drug lords? Were you that desperate to get back in the game?" I asked.

"Yes." Jack slammed his right fist into his open left palm, a real act of emotion for him. I looked at the mountains to the west trying to control my rage.

"What do you want me to do for you, Jack?" I felt numb. My head was throbbing and I wanted to scream at him.

He turned to me with a pained look on his face, his lips trembling. "Get my money back! I don't care how. Just do it. I know how you operate. You can do things the police can't. I don't care how you do it, just do it."

"I'll look into it. If the money is accessible I'll get it, but no guarantees, okay?" I said.

We shook hands and started walking back down the runway toward the burned-out helicopters. There was a movement behind the wreckage of one of them and I started to reach for the Glock in my ankle holster when I saw Deputy Woo's face pop up over the instrument panel. He climbed out and came toward us.

"What's up, Woo?" I asked. He had something in his hand.

"Cartridges from an AK-47. Found two of them off in the grass. FBI missed them, lucky us, huh?"

"Depends on what you have."

"I got two 7.62 millimeter casings, armory marks indicate Prague, Czechoslovakia, but they're reloads, see?" He held up one of the empty casings. "The necks aren't fully crimped and you can see the die marks on the outside of the casings. They're straight, no crimp, and the primers are a different color, brand new, and they aren't fully seated. That happens when you hand load these things. The shell casings have extra thick walls. They're tough to reload on a hand press but that's what was done here. See the scratches?"

"Why would they do that?" asked Jack.

"Because they didn't have access to a supply of factory ammo for the AK-47," Kim replied.

"Which means they're amateurs, right?" Jack said.

"Maybe," answered Woo, "or they are mercenaries on the fringe. We saw alot of these groups in Angola and Somalia. They operated for months on their own, working for one side or the other."

"Any ideas where they came from, where they went, who they were and are they really terrorists?" I asked.

"I would have to guess but there are a lot of possibilities. They might be Cubans out of Algeria. The lizard shoes, the hand-loaded cartridges, the Huggre slacks which are French and are found all over West Africa, the accents and Latino characteristics. It all points to Cuban mercenaries. Many of them went to Algeria for sanctuary after the Angolan war cooled off, and they operate out of training camps there whenever someone will pay their fee. It's better than going back to Cuba where they would have to work in the fields to earn a living. Since the Soviets stopped their support to Cuba there is no easy life for these mercenaries. Let's face it, since 1962 when the Soviets moved into Cuba for real, the Cuban mercenary groups have had it pretty good. Some of them haven't seen their homeland since the early 1970's when they were shipped around the world to support leftist revolutions."

"This all sounds right and I agree it's a wild guess, but what connects this group with the Cubans you described?" I asked.

"Oh, yes, there is one more thing." He held the two casings up and pointed to the bases. "See those little paint spots on the bottoms? One has a little dab of red paint and the other has a blue spot. That clinches it for me. The Cuban mercenaries used to mark their cartridges like that so each squad would know their own ammo. After an engagement they would go back and police the area for spent casings so they could reload them. We would go back too. It was always a turkey shoot until they caught on and started hiring local children to do their scavenging."

"Doesn't sound like a very well organized revolution. How can anyone fight a war with recycled ammo and Latinos wearing lizard shoes and French designer pants?" I asked.

"Don't underestimate these guys, O'Keefe. They know how to survive and they can fight if they have to. You surprised them last night, but don't count on doing it again. You were right when you said they'd be back. Whoever is behind this is just a bit crazy. Staging a robbery with AK-47s, Italian helicopters and a blown safe with nitro is too obvious. In Europe or the Middle East it would just be considered part of the ongoing terrorist activity of the region. They over-did it here. They could have waited until everyone was asleep and then open the safe with an electronic pic and no one would have known the difference. I think you're right, they were just thugs and they probably aren't above revenge."

"Maybe I'm dense, gentlemen," said Jack, "but I don't get it. What is the connection between Cuban mercenaries, robbery, and top secret government documents?"

"I think I can answer that," I said. "If they used local muscle, it would tip us off who was behind this so they imported these Cuban mercenaries to make it look like a terrorist operation. They were available and cheap. Add the AK-47s, the helicopters and the explosives, and we were supposed to overlook the robbery of the guests. So, we should look for a local connection, someone who has a lot to lose if that report is implemented. Someone who has a weird sense of humor and very little class."

"That would describe half the people I know," said Jack.

"Yes, but, there's one more element here we haven't touched on, and that's the timing." I said.

"Yes," Kim pointed out the obvious. "Why did they stage the robbery and blow the safe when they did? It had to be timing."

"Jack said he hadn't read the report. It was still sealed in the safe, right Jack?" He nodded in the affirmative. "They didn't want you to see it. You were supposed to meet right after the fireworks to discuss it and then everyone would have known its contents. They had to get it out of the safe and away before you saw it," I said.

"You mean someone who was in that room last night did that?" Jack, asked, a look of horror on his face.

"Yes, someone in that room or someone who was supposed to be there. I wouldn't trust anyone right now if I were you and that includes those FBI people in there. Someone with a lot of power and influence is behind this," I said.

"That's for sure," said Kim.

"Oh, no!" Jack said, shaking his head.

We left Woo to his investigation and returned to the main house. The morning was your average summer day: bright and sunny, warming fast, burning the dew off the grass, with high thin clouds moving in from the west. It was a beautiful day and it was time to go.

"I'll do some digging for your money and see what happens, Jack. Sometimes, when you turn over a rock, all kinds of things crawl out into the light of day. Can't promise anything but I'll give it my best shot."

"Thanks, we'll be back in two months. If you need me, just call this number and I'll get right back to you. It's sort of an international beeper service." He handed me a card.

We shook hands and Jack walked into the greenhouse. I went around the side of the house toward Connie's car. As I walked, I heard a noise and looked up to find Timothy and Jonathan leaning out their second story bedroom window. Samantha was behind them peering over their shoulders.

"Hi Dad...We didn't change our minds. They made us stay," mumbled Timothy. Jonathan and Samantha were both crying.

"Yeah," Jonathan sobbed, "we miss you."

"It's going to be all right, guys," I said. "I'll be back. Be good till then. If you need me, I'll come any time."

I gave them the thumbs up and walked away before I made a complete fool of myself. Little did I know how important those last words would become in the days that followed.

CHAPTER TWELVE

I GAVE THE CHILDREN A wave as we circled the house. We passed through the two large fieldstone pillars with attached wrought iron gates that marked the entrance to the estate. I'd never seen the gates closed and wondered if they would even turn on their rusty hinges. After all, what's the use of having gates if you don't use them?

"That was a rotten trick that your ex-wife and her mother played on those kids. I was really looking forward to spending some time with them, especially little Samantha," Connie said.

"They're a very manipulative pair and I've learned not to buck them. They're determined to control the children's destiny," I said.

"And everyone else's as well...Oh, I am sorry, Bill, but it just really makes me angry to see what she does. How can you stand it? Do you see what I mean? I don't want to sound like a complainer, but it's just too much."

"I suppose I run away from it. I go to the sailboat or my cottage in the dunes, and I stay away from people until I'm able to cope again. I've learned the hard way not to fight with either of them. They don't fight fair, and if you win they lay in ambush forever until they get back at you."

"So, win or lose, no matter how you play the game, you lose."

"Right!"

"Wow that is a tough way to live for anyone, especially three young children," she said.

"Don't underestimate those kids. They're pretty resilient," I said.

We were winding our way down the mountain on the narrow blacktop road, fields and woods on either side with an occasional old farmhouse set back in the trees. I took my time, being especially careful on the curves. I saw the broken telephone pole, the downed wires, the sheared off trees, and pieces of glass and metal scattered along the side of the road and I knew what it was before Connie even spoke.

"Look, Bill, someone must have had an accident."

"Not really, Babe," I responded. "It was no accident."

We rounded the curve and saw the wreckage of the chopper on the far side of a small hay field to the right smashed against a rock wall and some large mountain oak trees. Cars were parked along the side of the road and into the field where three police cars formed a barrier around the crash site, keeping the sightseers away from the wreckage. The pilot had made a valiant effort to put it down in the open field, but lost control when the chopper hit the trees and telephone pole coming in. Connie was silent as I slowed to a crawl and made my way past the parked cars and people in the road.

"Do you want to stop and have a look see, Tiger?" she said.

"No, I don't think so." I said, not looking.

"What a horrible way to die, and you did all that?"

"Yeah! I did it. It's all my fault," I said as I stepped on the gas.

We rode in silence for a while. The traffic was light so I took Rt. 9 down the east side of the Hudson River to Tarrytown; then Rt. 287 across to White Plains and the headquarters building of Daylight Inns, the company for which Connie worked. She was Vice President of Standards and Compliance and was required to be available twenty-four hours a day. The company provided her with a penthouse suite on the top floor of their headquarters. The city's zoning ordinance restricted buildings to four stories, so the view from Connie's porch was one of the New York Central Railroad tracks now called the Metro North. This was not very exciting but it was a good deal for Connie who was considered one of the top candidates in line for promotion in the company. We were talking again when we reached her place.

"Wanna come up for some lunch and a little making out?" she

asked.

"Don't mind if I do, but what will management think about you bringing in outside help?"

"I'll tell them you're a consultant and I need guidance with some techniques we plan to use in our newer hotels so our customers will feel more at home and relaxed."

"I hope this doesn't cost me anything. I'm a little short after all the excitement last night."

"We'll have to see what we can do about that," she chided and began to get playful.

"You better wait till we get upstairs, or we may embarrass the security guy watching the cameras," I said.

"They won't even know it. We'll use the executive elevator. It opens right out onto my floor, and no one will even see us."

I pulled around the back of the building to the basement entrance and used Connie's pass card to open the gate to the executive parking area. The building was a typically modern square-concrete-no-imagination-building with a flat roof and a lot of glass. We went down a ramp and made a couple of turns following signs which read "Executives Only".

"This is really neat. We should do this more often," I said as we rode the Executive Elevator up to the top floor. "I can really get off on sneaking around here with my girlfriend."

"I've noticed that you get off on the strangest things, Bill. If you prefer, you can keep coming in the front entrance, but this is the way we do it after hours. Besides, I think we deserve some privacy. I need a break from people for awhile."

"Yes, things have been really intense. Maybe you need to be alone?" I asked.

"No, of course not, dummy. You're always welcome." Connie put her arms around my neck and showed me how welcome I was. We were really getting into it when the elevator door opened and we came face to face with a security guard, his hand on the butt of his revolver. He was about 5' 9", maybe 200 pounds, very much out of shape and he looked twice my age.

"Oh! It's you, Miss Wilson...ahh...is everything all right?" he asked.

"Yes, of course it is, Herb. Why wouldn't it be?"

"Well...ahh...I'm sorry to do this but we had a problem and I'm gonna hafta check on all visitors." He pointed to me. "I'm really sorry but I gotta check you out, fella."

He stepped back against the far wall as we left the elevator with his hand still on his gun. It was holstered and the safety strap was snapped across the back of the hammer. Lucky for him I wasn't a bad guy. The old man was trying to do a man-sized job but he no longer had the tools.

"It's all right, Herb," said Connie. "This is Mr. O'Keefe, a very close friend of mine. I'll vouch for him."

"Sorry, Miss Wilson. I got my orders. Mr. Delmar himself says I gotta search all unknowns. This fella could be forcing you to bring him here against your will." Connie giggled. "If you get hurt, it would all be my fault." He was very serious.

"It's okay, Herb," I said. "Go ahead and search me. Where would you like me to stand...how about over here, facing the wall, okay?"

"Oh, no, that's not necessary," he said. "I'll just check you out right where you stand."

I opened my sports jacket for him to see there was nothing under it, and he went through the formality of patting me down. He missed the Glock on my left ankle and the Special Forces knife on my right. He was too fat to bend down that far. When he finished, he was breathing in short gasps, his face was red and he was sweating.

"Now tell us, if you will, what is going on around here Herb."

"I'm sorry, Miss Wilson. You'll hafta talk to Mr. Delmar. He's in your apartment right now. We had a break-in last night. He'll tell ya all about it," he said, wheezing as he breathed.

We continued down the hallway, our footsteps muffled by the plush gray shag carpet. The recessed ceiling lights washed gently over the beige walls, interrupted every few feet by some piece of modern art framed in chrome; someone's idea of power decorating. At the end of the corridor we turned left for a short way then right and came to the open door of Connie's apartment.

"Oh no! The place is a disaster, Bill. Everything is broken and messed up." She began to cry as a man came to the door.

"Connie! Thank God, you're all right. Where have you been? We've been looking all over. I didn't even know you were gone."

He took her hand, put his arm around her shoulder, and led her inside. I followed dutifully into the living room. The picture windows on the west side of the apartment had been smashed. Furniture and walls were riddled by bullet holes. Shell casings lay scattered everywhere. I saw no blood but this was obviously not just an ordinary break-in. Connie was talking to Delmar, a slim, medium sized version of a Fifth Avenue male model. Everything about the man was perfection.

"...But, John! How could they have gotten in so easily?"

"It wasn't that easy, Connie," he said. "There were four of them. They came down on parachutes and landed on the roof. They dropped ropes, rappelled down the side of the building, smashed the windows, and came in shooting." Delmar looked at me, measuring my reaction. "Went straight for your bedroom and pulverized the bed. Needless to say, they expected you to be there." He threw a not too friendly glance my way again.

"I...I don't understand," mumbled Connie. "Why?" Tears poured down her face as she sat on the edge of the couch and buried her face in her hands. Delmar turned to me.

"You're O'Keefe, right? She was with you, I take it?"

He was thin in the shoulders, early fifties, slightly balding, with an expensive light brown suit and hand crafted Italian shoes. His officious manner put me off and I didn't like him so I just turned and walked to the windows where two workmen were busy replacing the glass in the picture windows. The outside was a four-story drop, straight down, no handholds. The four ropes were still there.

"You say they came in on parachutes?" I asked.

"Yes, one of the guards thought he heard a helicopter, and then the roof alarms went off. They're calibrated for ninety-five pounds so the dogs won't set them off. They're pressure release alarms, state of the art, can't have laser beams or trip wires because of the birds you know." Delmar warmed to his subject. "After the alarms went off, we released the dogs, Dobermans, none better, and two guards went to the roof. By the time they got there, the intruders had already broken in here and started shooting. The guards rushed down here, but by then it was all over. They were gone."

"So, you're telling me your security guards were up there when the intruders were in here, and your men left the grapples and ropes in place and came running down to see what was happening here?"

"Well...ahh...yes. I suppose that's one way of putting it. They thought it was more important to confront the intruders and apprehend them. Our security staff is very well trained you know."

"They messed up. They should have tossed the ropes and then the intruders would have been trapped. They could have bottled them up and called for backup. Very simple operation but your guards are not trained for this kind of intrusion. It's not their fault."

"I must disagree with you, Mr. O'Keefe." Delmar's face was beet red. "Our security is the best. Our guards are trained at our central school in Chicago. John Chusak is the director and he would not take kindly to being criticized by an amateur like you. No one could possibly have guessed this would happen. My God...it's…so… frightening." He choked back a sob and looked at me helplessly.

"But why?" asked Connie joining us at the windows. "Do you think this is connected with the robbery at the Sullivan's estate last night, Bill?"

"Robbery? There was a robbery where you were last night?" Delmar stared wide-eyed at Connie.

"It was nothing," I said. "I don't think the two are connected."

I gave Connie a hard warning glance to shut her up. I wanted information, not hysterical speculation. A lot of things didn't make sense and one of them was Delmar, so I decided to test him.

"Have the police been here yet?"

"Oh...no. There's no need for police. The company would prefer not to indulge in that sort of publicity. I've been in contact with Chicago and my instructions are to clean it up."

I knew something about the corporate setup of Daylight Inns, because Connie and I had been spending a lot of time together since we met the previous summer. Daylight Inns was a subsidiary of ATI (American Telex International), which was solely owned by CFI (Continental Financial International). Mr. Delmar would have much to explain when his superiors got the report on this one and I was not about to help him.

"Jack Chusak is on his way from Chicago to do the investigation personally," said Delmar. "He's the best and he has a team of scientists who can do all the forensics work, maybe even better than the FBI. That's why we left the ropes in place, so he can see what really happened when he arrives."

There were cleanup people all over the place, sweeping and vacuuming, hauling loads of debris out the door. I picked up a few shell casings and put them in a plastic sandwich bag.

"Maybe we shouldn't clean the place up until Mr. Chusak arrives," Connie suggested.

"Oh, don't worry, Jack is smart. He can figure out what went on here without having to see all this mess. Besides, we took pictures, and since no one got hurt, it's not a big deal."

Delmar was just interested in covering up. I knew John Chusak, Jack to his friends. I did some work for him and Continental Financial when I was with my partner, Willie Monk. That was before Willie suffered a stroke one day walking on the beach at my place. Jack wouldn't be happy about the cleanup job. He was a hands-on guy. He liked to see it for himself.

"I'm hungry. Any ideas where we can find something to eat around here?" I asked.

"The refrigerator and cabinets were destroyed," said Delmar. "The employees cafeteria is closed today and there's nothing else in the building except some candy machines. I would invite you over to my place, but Lydia and the kids are at her mother's in New London for the week, so maybe you can find a place on Main Street. There are some nice restaurants in town. I'll stay here and wait for John if you want to go out for awhile."

"Sounds good to me," I said as I grabbed Connie's hand and pulled her toward the door.

We rode, without talking, down the same elevator in which we had come up. Finally, Connie broke the silence.

"Would it not be easier if we took your car, Bill? After all, it's right outside in the parking lot and mine is low on gas."

"I don't think we should go near my car right now."

"Why? It's been there since yesterday morning and you always say it should be started everyday or the battery gets low."

"Because that's how they found us, babe."

"Who?"

"My car has been parked out front of this building since yesterday morning when we went up to the Sullivan's. That's how they found us. They thought we were inside your apartment. They didn't know we were still at the estate."

"But who could that possibly be?" she asked.

"Someone who doesn't like me," I said, checking the Glock.

CHAPTER THIRTEEN

WE RODE WITHOUT TALKING. Connie was silent, showing no reaction to the destruction of her home and that worried me. She had been through enough trauma the past two days to put anyone over the edge. We found a small Chinese restaurant off the main street of the downtown area, not a place you'd take your mother, but the food was good. Connie called John Delmar from a pay phone in the back corner to ask if she could bring him something. He said he would call back but he didn't. Just as we were about to dig into a pile of Moo Goo Gai Pan and a double order of hot steaming pork-fried rice, John Chusak walked in the door, pulled up a chair, and sat down.

"Can we talk O'Keefe?" He was not the friendly Jack I'd always known, although his appearance hadn't changed much. He had dark wavy hair, a deeply lined face, a sports shirt open at the throat, sneakers, and jeans complimented by a tweed sports jacket. He was in his late fifties, older than John Delmar, but he wore it well.

"I'll talk any time, but right now I'm about to stuff my face with hot greasy monosodium glutamate. Wanna join us?"

He looked at my plate, nodded and said, "Why not?" and I filled him in while we ate.

"So tell me why they broke into Connie's apartment and blew everything away? What were they really looking for?" he asked.

"I'll give you everything I know but I have to have your solemn promise it will remain absolutely confidential, that you will tell no one and make no records of our conversation," I said.

"Get real, O'Keefe. You sound like James Bond 007, and all that stuff. Is it really all that serious?"

"You saw Connie's apartment. Is that serious enough? You tell me."

"Yeah, okay, but I gotta tell ya this terrorist thing doesn't make sense."

"You're right, it doesn't unless you know about SARTXE."

"What? Tex? What the hell is that?"

"I'll tell you, Jack, but it has to remain between us."

"All right, so I promise on my scout's honor. Lay it on me."

"It goes back to when I was working at the New York City office of State Mutual. Willie Monk was their chief investigator. He never went to college but he could do things with a computer I've never seen anyone else do since. One day he showed me something he found while hacking around on the company system. It was an entry for a ten percent consulting fee paid to a company named SARTXE Inc. with a Chicago address. When he tried to trace the address, he found it didn't exist. He'd run across this before and was never able to find out who SARTXE was, but if you will notice," I took out my pen and wrote on a paper napkin, "the name is EXTRAS spelled backwards.

Willie thought maybe this was some sort of joke until he added up the amount of money paid out to this account by different companies and he realized it was in the millions. He was looking at a very sophisticated kickback system on major contracts being funded by many of the leading insurance companies in the country."

"You gotta be kidding. How'd they cover it up?"

"Computer magic. Willie would find a reference to SARTXE, and track it but the thing would disappear, wiped out and covered up. Millions were siphoned off through electronic transfers, and then written off under other categories as miscellaneous disbursements, so there was never any permanent record of the payments. We chased SARTXE all over the place, watched it appear and disappear until we thought we'd lose our minds."

"Are you pulling my leg?" said Jack, scooping up the last of the pork fried rice.

"We went on our own when the company let him go. They said they wanted only college graduates, so Willie got his walking papers and I went with him. We formed a partnership and that's when you came to know us. I sometimes wonder if the real reason Willie was let out was because he was too good. Maybe he was getting too close to something really big."

"Like SARTXE?"

"Yes, then Willie got sick and went into the nursing home. My wife divorced me because I was no longer respectable, and I continued working alone as an insurance investigator. I met Connie last year in East Harbour out on Long Island during a very messy insurance fraud and murder scheme worth six million dollars."

"I remember that, but the money was never found and a lot of people ended up dead. Your name was mentioned as the investigator who cracked the case, but there were some nasty accusations about the methods you used."

"I messed up the plans of some very important people in East Harbour. There were several references to SARTXE in that case and I prevented the payoffs from being made. I made some real big time enemies and now I walk around armed at all times."

"So, you believe it was SARTXE that made the hit on Connie's apartment this morning. But why there?"

"My car was parked outside the building. Whoever was watching probably didn't see us leave out the back exit of the parking garage in Connie's car."

"So, you're saying they thought you were in her apartment?"

"Yes, and they wanted to make an example of us to warn everyone not to mess with SARTXE. Very effective, huh?"

"But why would the assault on Connie's apartment not be the same people who pulled the robbery at your in-laws' estate? They both used helicopters, assault rifles and terrorist techniques." Jack said as he commandeered the last of the Moo Goo Gai Pan.

"There are some similarities but the differences are more important. They both used helicopters, but the group that hit Connie's place escaped by land transport and they had different weapons. At the Sullivan's estate last night, they used AK-47s with reloaded ammo from Czechoslovakia."

"The four gunners that hit Connie's apartment used automatic weapons but they were made in the U.S.A., as was the ammo. Both groups were imported but they operated differently. The Latinos at the Sullivan's estate were unsophisticated thugs interested in robbery and murder. They were not well organized and they were poorly disciplined. The four who parachuted onto the top of the Daylight Inn building were highly trained and well disciplined. They stuck with their mission, did their job and were gone before anyone could stop them."

"Yes, I've seen their kind before," said Chusak.

"So have I."

"Will somebody please let me in on what's going on here?" asked Connie as she nibbled on a fortune cookie.

Jack and I said the same words in unison, "Navy Seals!"

"Yeah, Navy Seals, just their kind of operation. Probably retired types working on contract," said Jack.

"I'm not so sure they're retired," I said, pulling several shell casings out of my jacket pocket. "Have a look at these."

Chusak took the shell casings and examined them. The frown on his face became one of astonishment as he turned them around, lifting each to the light to read the markings on the bases.

"Holy Geronimo, you're right! I haven't seen one of these since the early days of Viet Nam. Stoners! Only the Navy Seals had them and boy, did they do a lot of damage with these babies."

"Delmar picked up all the shell casings," I said.

"Yeah, I dropped by the apartment. Cleaning it up doesn't help me do my job. I wanted to see the entry tracks and dispersion patterns of spent shell casings. Now I'll have trouble with all of that."

"It was Delmar's idea. Sorry about that, Jack," Connie said.

"Delmar is a sponge. He can't go to the toilet alone without permission. You can be sure he's doing exactly as he was told, which means my coming here was just a sham to make things look good. When I get back to Chicago, Delmar will be lucky to see another sunrise if I have anything to say about it."

"Trust no one!" I said.

"And take no prisoners," said Chusak.

"Damn right!" we echoed in unison.

"Again, gentlemen," said Connie, "What's going on?"

"Oh, sorry," I said. "You see, these shell casings came from a weapon called a Stoner-50. The Armalite Corporation made the Stoner during Viet Nam, and only the Navy Seals had them. The designer was Eugene Stoner and he liked the smaller caliber 5.56mm bullet with its high velocity, which produced hydrostatic shock. They were outfitted to carry one hundred fifty rounds with a left hand feed. A squad of Seals was an awesome and lethal fighting unit. By the way, Jack, the shell casings were being collected and put into plastic bags by Delmar's boys. Maybe they're still around."

"Don't worry, my men will see to it things are done right." He turned and said, "The worst of it is, Connie, even to this day, only the Navy Seals carry the Stoner or stock this ammo."

"That means that these were real Navy Seals that tried to kill us?" Connie's lower lip was trembling. "Oh no!"

Pretty scary, isn't it folks?" said Chusak. "We may be dealing with something very big. You're right, O'Keefe, real James Bond stuff. If it is this SARTXE that we're dealing with, they really have some connections."

The food was gone and we concentrated on the fortune cookies. Jack's said there was romance in his future. Connie's mentioned financial success, mine said I'd have an adventure soon.

"That's an understatement," Connie jibed.

We returned to Connie's apartment where Chusak's team of investigators was crawling all over the place, taking samples, snapping pictures, vacuuming up evidence, and checking for fingerprints. I knew what they would find and it wouldn't be much, but they had a job to do, if for no other reason than to save face.

"Do you have a bomb expert with you, Jack?" I asked.

"Yes, one of the best, Jimmy Daniels. Why?"

"Could you have him look my car over? I have a bad feeling about it." I handed him my keys.

"Consider it done."

I helped Connie pack up her personal belongings and then, using the pictures Delmar took, we went over the entry tracks and dispersion patterns of shell casings with Chusak. He was a pro and

I liked working with him. Most industrial security people are not equipped to handle incidents like this, but Jack was different. He'd been an intelligence officer in the Army, a Chicago police detective, and then a security analyst with Daylight Inns. He climbed the ladder to the top at Continental Financial which was no small feat. He'd seen his share of murder scenes and bullet holes in walls. I watched as he methodically progressed from one end of the apartment to the other, making notes as he went.

"What we got here is a real smooth operation," he said. "No brand names on the parachutes or ropes, no fingerprints, no cigarette butts, no nothing, just the shell casings and they're clean too. Geeze, five hundred twenty-seven rounds fired in less than a minute. That's what my boys counted. What kind of a world do we live in?"

"A very complex and dangerous world. You seem surprised by all this," I said.

"I'm always surprised by the antics of my fellow man. I was just thinking what it must have been like in here when the fireworks went off. It was dark but those four shooters let off five hundred twenty-seven rounds and never hit each other with a single shot. Then I was thinking what it would be like waking up as the target of all that firepower. Not a very pleasant thought. I'm just thankful no one was in that bedroom. This is going to be difficult enough to explain without bodies. I'm not sure where to go from here," he said looking very tired.

"I have some ideas," I said, "and I need your help, but you may want to think carefully about it before you answer."

He nodded and said, "What is it you want and don't be so mysterious. We've known each other long enough not to play games, O'Keefe."

"You're right, so can you trace some names for me? I know you have the data banks to do it, but if you start digging around, you could stir up a hornet's nest."

"Look, I don't scare easily. Are you saying I'll draw fire from these people if I help you?"

"Something like that, yes, but I don't have many options and time is critical."

"Don't worry, I've been a target before. I'd like to nail these jokers, so what do you want?" he asked, a glint of fire in his eyes. I gave him the names and suggested a few possibilities. I had too many problems to solve and not much time and I had to consider the safety of my family and Connie while I tried to track down the documents stolen from Jack Sullivan's safe. I had the problem of Jack's money and what Jersey Mutual had done with it. I also had a personal mission to track down SARTXE, four Navy Seals, and the renegade Latinos with AK-47s. They went too far when they blasted Connie's apartment. Enough is enough already!

"Hey, Bill, come here." Jack was standing at the door. Another man stood in the hallway with something in his hands.

"This is Billy Daniels, our bomb expert," said Chusak, "and this is a bomb he just found under the hood of your car."

Like I said, "Enough is enough!"

CHAPTER FOURTEEN

WE LEFT CHUSAK AND Delmar in the wreckage of Connie's apartment, the two of them nose to nose in a tense confrontation over control of the investigation.

"I want this apartment sealed off until further notice," yelled Chusak. "I don't want any more workmen or maintenance people in here until I say so, and if you need confirmation from Chicago, buster, you'll get it."

"I have my instructions too, Chusak. You'll see that they come from pretty high up, so don't threaten me unless you're ready to risk your job, Buddy Boy," yelled Delmar.

I think the "Buddy Boy" might have done it because Chusak took Delmar by his throat and walked him into the bedroom, slamming the door behind them.

"Well, Tiger, what's next?" asked Connie as we rode the elevator to the ground floor. "You got us kicked out of the Sullivan estate because of your cave man act. Then you get my apartment wasted so we can't stay there. After Chusak gets through with Delmar I may not even have a job. This vagabond life you lead becomes more interesting all the time."

"Stick with me, sweetheart. The best is yet to come," I said, opening the trunk of my Caddy.

"Is this car safe to drive, Bill? Are you sure they got all the bombs?"

she asked.

"We'll find out soon enough." I turned the key and the engine started without any problems. No explosions, no big booming noises, no fireballs.

"Well, I guess we're safe," said Connie.

"Not really. The bomb they found under the hood was equipped with a single throw mercury motion activated switch. That means nothing happens until you step on the brake and the momentum throws the mercury forward in the tube tripping the switch, causing contact and...BOOM!"

"So, you're saying we aren't really safe until you step on the brakes?"

"You got it, Sherlock."

"Well do it so we can get on with the rest of our lives," she said.

So, I put it in gear and started up, then stepped on the brakes and nothing happened.

"Thanks!" she said curling up to sleep in the passenger seat. It was nice to have the old Connie back again.

She was right, there weren't many places we could go. Our options were limited to the cottage on the eastern end of Long Island and my sailboat also on the Island. We could go to a hotel or a bed and breakfast, but I refused to run away into hiding. So I headed for my cottage located on a wildlife refuge in the dunes. I took the Throgs Neck Bridge, picked up the Long Island Expressway and settled in for the drive. It was almost midnight and traffic was light, but I tried to stay alert. They probably wouldn't make another attempt on our lives so soon, but there was no sense in taking chances.

I took the LIE to its end, then Main Road up the North Fork, and by the time I reached the turnoff to my cottage the moon was high in its track across the summer night sky. I followed the dirt road across my neighbor's potato field into a stand of tall pines, to a turnaround at the gate to the wildlife refuge. Granddad O'Keefe built the place, and when it was turned into a nature preserve he kept the cottage for his own use. No cars were allowed, so I parked at the turnaround and we walked the rest of the way to the cottage, about three hundred yards. It was early morning and I was tired. I had experienced more excitement during the past two days than any man could stand, so all

I wanted was to crawl into bed and sleep.

We left our suitcases in the car and began the walk through the moonlit sand-scape with a flashlight: dunes all around us, the sound of the surf pounding up ahead beyond the shadowy form of the cottage, the squawking of an occasional gull breaking the eerie silence of the night. The wind was on shore, and that brought the first clue that all was not well. It was a familiar stench, one that I thought I'd left behind in the jungles and hoped never to encounter again. I doused the light, pulled the Glock, and led Connie off to the left around a series of low sand dunes to the front of the cottage.

"The front door of the cottage is open," Connie said. "Oooh, what's that smell? Bill, I'm scared." She put her hand on my arm.

"Stay here and wait for me, Babe. I'll check it out."

I moved forward keeping a low profile, checking all around for signs of life but there were none. The only thing I found was my neighbor, George Willis, president of the North Fork Watch Committee, lying in the sand. He was very dead, garroted by the neck, his eyes bulging out at me accusingly. I could almost hear his voice from the past chiding me so many times for allowing strangers onto the refuge in violation of the many rules governing its existence. Now his worries were over forever.

I moved to the front door and flashed the light inside. All was quiet but the place was a mess. On the floor of the living room lay George's wife, Ginny, but she wasn't alone and the story was obvious. She must have discovered the man dressed in a light tan suit in my cottage. He'd tried to strangle her, but before he succeeded she managed to grab a butcher knife and stabbed him several times. His hands were around her neck and she still held the handle of the butcher knife embedded in his chest. They had been dead awhile. I left them and returned to the place where Connie was waiting.

"What's going on, Bill? What took you so long?" she hugged me.

"Not a pretty sight in there, Connie. We have three dead bodies. Let's get out of here." I wasn't feeling well.

We backtracked the way we came to keep the area clean of tracks. My cell phone was dead and Connie's was in her apartment. I tried the car phone but it didn't work, probably disconnected by the bomb expert, so we drove up to Henry Coddlestone's house. His potato fields surrounded the wildlife preserve. I was reluctant to start banging on anyone's front door at such an early hour, so I just stopped the car in the front yard with the engine running and the high beams trained on the house. I thought someone would eventually wake up and come to the door. My window was open for fresh air and I was watching the house when suddenly I felt something cold and hard against my left ear.

"Don't move," said a low raspy voice. "Put your hands on the steering wheel and don't move a muscle."

"Okay...Henry. Is that you, Henry? It's me, O'Keefe. For crying out loud man, it's me." I put my hands up.

Henry lowered the shotgun and moved around beside the car. He had evidently gone out the back door of the farmhouse and around the car with his double-barreled shotgun in hand.

"What the hell are you doin' in my front yard at four o'clock in the mornin', Billy? I thought you was some kook from the city lookin' for a place to do some spoonin'. Turn off your engine and come on in. Martha will have breakfast ready soon and you're welcome."

My experience with farmers has always been the same. They handle any crisis with laconic efficiency. If someone wakes you up at four o'clock in the morning, just stick a gun to his head and then invite him to breakfast.

I filled Henry in on what I'd found at my cottage and then used his telephone to call the state police. Martha threw together a quick breakfast of buckwheat cakes, eggs, bacon, orange juice, coffee, and muffins. Then she packed us some sausage and biscuit sandwiches to go just in case we got hungry later on. When the police cars and ambulances started to arrive, Henry decided to go with us to meet them. We thanked Martha and left.

"George and Ginny Willis were good friends." That is all he said but I noticed his eyes were watering.

Four state troopers and a sheriff's deputy were waiting at the turnaround. I briefed them on what I found and showed them the track I took going and coming. The oldest of the group, a Sergeant Cummings, took charge at the cottage.

"We'll wait outside for the Lieutenant," he said. "Don't want to mess anything up."

He started taping off the area and told me to wait at the turnaround. That was all right with me. I'd already seen enough death. It was time to sit back and let someone else take the lead.

CHAPTER FIFTEEN

THE SUN BROKE LOW on the eastern horizon a half hour later and Lieutenant Hank Gaines, sporting a day old beard surrounding a big yawn, arrived in his dark green unmarked sedan. Hank and I went back a long way. We were buddies in Viet Nam.

"You've got no right to do this to me, O'Keefe, you SOB," he said as he stifled a big yawn. "I still have a stack of paperwork on my desk from last year what with that East Harbour business. Now you're at it again. I'm telling you right now Buddy, we ain't buddies no more. All bets are off. From now on you owe me." He stretched his arms and let out a deep groan. So much for friendship.

"You always this pleasant in the morning, Hank, or haven't you had your first cup of coffee?" I handed him one of Martha's sausage biscuits. "Here, try this. It'll cure the early morning blahs."

"What's this?" He unwrapped it, held it up to the light, gave it a quick sniff and took a big bite.

"Wow, that's good. Where'd you get this? I haven't had one of these since I was a kid."

"Got it from Martha Coddlestone, farmer's wife on the left as you come in. Here, have another."

"Don't mind if I do." We started walking to the cottage and I filled him in as we went, warning him what he was about to see."

"Man, O'Keefe, if I live to be a thousand, I'll never get used to the smell of death. I got three more years to retirement, and maybe I'll make it if you stop calling me every time you get into trouble."

"I didn't do this one, Hank. These are my neighbors and I never intended for them to get hurt. I want whoever did this and I want them bad. They need to know they can't get away with this sort of thing. This is America, not Baghdad. There has to be an end to people who think they can kill and maim without paying for it."

"You sound like a politician, Billy."

"Yeah, sometimes I surprise myself."

"Tell you what, friend," said Hank, "what say we stand up wind over there on the beach while the coroner and forensics boys do their stuff. Those sausage biscuits don't taste so hot any more."

I told Hank about the fireworks and robbery at the Sullivan's estate on the Fourth of July, and about Connie's apartment and Jack Chusak on the fifth of July in White Plains.

"Now it's the sixth of July and we've got these three corpses, and you think this is connected to that East Harbour scam from last year?" asked Hank.

"Not sure, but my old boss, John Stanley, president of State Mutual, threatened to get me and this has all the signs of a well planned hit. These guys came here, and when they didn't find me, somebody probably checked Connie's place where my car was parked outside. They didn't know we were gone, so they pulled a raid on Connie's apartment at the Daylight Inns Headquarters building, thinking that a holiday weekend would be a good time since all the employees would be gone. The car bomb was just a backup in case they missed."

"If those were Navy Seals with Stoners, like you think, then this SARTXE has got some real clout some place high up. You don't just borrow a team like that or dial up the number in the yellow pages. A Seal team works together for years before they develop that sort of precision. They know each other and how they think and act, so when they go into a hot spot, they don't blow away their buddies."

"A lot like we were in Nam, right?" I added.

"Yeah, a lot like us. I guess it never goes away does it, Billy? Hey man, I'm sorry. You know what I said before? I didn't mean it, okay? We still buddies?"

"Sure." We high-fived and started back to the cottage.

The coroner's team was removing the bodies, but the smell remained. I would have to renovate the place after this one. The coroner came over to us looking grim, his face white as snow.

"Sometimes this job isn't fun," he said.

"Bill O'Keefe, this is Doctor Danny Swartz, County Coroner," said Hank. We shook hands.

"The man was strangled from behind by a wire," Swartz began, "and then he was dragged off the porch into the sand as it happened. You can see where he thrashed his feet at the bottom of the stairs, and then they dragged him in the sand. The woman had the butcher knife from the matched set of knives in the rack over the kitchen sink. Personally, I would have chosen the boning knife. It's thinner and sharper, but the butcher knife did the job. The struggle started in the kitchen. You can see the trail of blood, and then they went into the living room. Bruises on the woman's neck show she was grabbed from behind, but she managed to turn around and got about ten stab wounds into her attacker as he strangled her. He obviously underestimated her strength. The last stab went through the heart and he died about the same time she did, horrible way to go. Probably happened late morning, let's say two days ago on the Fourth of July. I'll know more when I do the autopsies."

"Thanks Doc," said Hank. "I'll see you later."

I looked at the body of George Willis lying in the sand. He wore a pair of binoculars on a strap around his neck.

"George and Ginny came over here often for hours to watch birds," I said to Hank. "They were very zealous about protecting the wildlife refuge. They may have been sitting in the dunes when these people came in, and they probably confronted them. "

We went into the cottage, being careful to step around the pools of blood and the areas marked out for evidence by forensics.

"They didn't mess the place up too bad," said Hank. "Must not have been here very long."

Sergeant Cummings came into the room, a quizzical look on his face. "Hank, we got a real puzzler here." He held up a plastic evidence bag with a handgun in it. "A Smith and Wesson .357 magnum in a hip holster on the man inside here."

"What's so puzzling about that, Pete?" Hank asked.

"He had this slung under his left shoulder." He held up another bag with a submachine gun in it.

"An Uzi?"

"Yeah, and that ain't all. Here's his I.D. He was Sergeant Vitro Alexander, Chicago Police. There's his driver's license, pictures of the wife and kiddies, and his badge."

"Just a bit out of his jurisdiction. Is that all?" asked Hank.

"No, we got airline tickets, Chicago Midway to Providence and return, ticket stubs for a car and three passengers on the Cross Island Ferry with a reservation for a return trip on the 3:00 P.M. ferry, July 4th, reservation #122168. There's also an envelope with maybe twenty-five G's. Whoever this fellow was, he was well paid."

"Yes, and that was probably just a down payment," I said.

Sergeant Pete Cummings rolled his eyes and looked at me. "You must be a pretty important fella to rate this sort of treatment. I know some punks that'll do a job like this for under a thousand dollars."

"You get what you pay for, Pete. If you want quality murder, you gotta go to Chicago and pay big bucks," said Hank.

"Maybe I should ask for a transfer to Chicago," said Pete.

"You wouldn't like it. You have to kill little old ladies, and I know you could never do that," said Hank

"Yeah, you've got a point there. Man this is a dirty mess," Pete said.

"Did he have anything else on him, like a note pad, papers or a cell phone?" I asked.

"Funny you should mention that. He had a little black book. It's in the kitchen on the counter. I'll get it," Pete said.

The little black book was a combination yearly calendar and address book. I leafed through it quickly. Sergeant Alexander kept very thorough notes in his own simple-minded shorthand. One note caught my attention. It was a short entry on a Friday, June 28th, no mystery about it at all.

It read, "Call V.C.-11:00 AM", and there was a New York City telephone number. I flipped to the address section under "C" and found the same number next to Victor Cantrelli's name. I think my heart may have ceased working or at least skipped a few beats. I literally faded out because the next thing I remembered was Hank shaking me by the shoulders and yelling in my face.

"O'Keefe! Hey, man, are you in there? What's going on with you? I've been talkin' to you and you aren't there." He stopped shaking me and stared into my eyes.

"Yes, okay, Hank. I'm with you." I shook my head. I had to collect my thoughts, so I walked into the guest bedroom with its large twelve over twelve multi-paned windows facing south. I opened three of them, sat down in a wicker porch chair and took deep breaths of fresh, clean ocean air.

"What's up, pal? You look like you saw a ghost, man," Hank said, following me.

I showed him the entries and explained briefly my encounter with Senator Cantrelli at the Sullivan's estate on the Fourth of July. I didn't say anything about Jack Sullivan's personal situation.

"So you're saying Senator Cantrelli is mixed up in SARTXE?"

"I don't know, but it looks fishy. Why would a police sergeant from Chicago be calling a United States senator in New York just a week before he shows up dead in my living room, and the good senator shows up in the presence of a mysterious robbery involving a paramilitary unit with AK-47s and helicopters at my ex-father-in-law's house?"

"I know Cantrelli and the politics in Albany," said Hank. "If I so much as ask a question about him, my tail will be on fire and there won't be a fire truck big enough to put out the flames. Man, you sure have a way of making important enemies."

"You don't know the half of it, Hank," I said, looking at the book.

I flipped through the addresses to the "S" section and stopped at Sergeant Alexander's entry for SARTXE. There it was with a telephone number and address in Champaign, Illinois. I handed the book to him and watched his expression of surprise.

"Geeze, O'Keefe, this ties it. Victor Cantrelli and SARTXE. How the hell do I handle this?" Hank said.

"You don't, Hank. It's too hot to handle, so let me handle that end of it and you stick to the murder. I can just picture the Chief in Chicago when you ask him what his Sergeant was doing killing people in a cottage on Long Island, and who was with him and where are they now?"

"Yeah, I see your point. I stick to the murder and you stick to what you do best, which is antagonizing important and powerful people. Let me know if you need my help."

I kept scanning the pages of the book and came to an entry under "D" for John Delmar with a White Plains number. By now I wasn't surprised at anything. I took a piece of paper and copied all the information I needed and handed the book back to Hank.

"Stay tuned, Hank. This should be a good one," I said.

He shook my hand and left me sitting there thinking about what I'd gotten myself into: Victor Cantrelli, SARTXE, Navy Seals, John Delmar, lizard shoes, secret reports, and missing money, not to mention murder.

"Bill?" It was Connie. "Are you all right, Tiger? Hank Gaines told me you flipped out." She stood in the doorway, a look of concern on her face.

"Sit down, Babe. I'm okay. I just need some time to gather my thoughts. By the way don't stand in front of the windows," I said. "It may not be safe!"

CHAPTER SIXTEEN

WE CLEANED UP THE cottage and relaxed on the front porch. The incoming tide had brought a shift to a westerly breeze as the sun pushed toward noon and I was reminded that I hadn't slept or eaten.

"What say we get out of here and go to the sailboat?" I said. "We can stop at Gabby's Diner and grab a good home cooked meal along the way."

"Sounds good, I don't think I can stay here tonight. I can't take any more dead bodies and bullet holes. I'm due for a real vacation," Connie said, snuggling up to me.

My grandfather built the cottage on concrete pilings. He sunk an old iron safe, face up, in the top of one of those pilings and then covered it with flagstone around the fireplace. I opened the safe and took out my .44 Magnum and extra ammunition for both it and the Glock. I took an extra thousand dollars cash, locked the safe, and replaced the flagstone and rug. When we left, I locked the door and put the key under the mat. If someone wanted in, they wouldn't have to break anything.

We headed for Green's Marina located across from Shelter Island on Peconic Bay, stopping at Gabby's Diner on the way for a hearty lunch of baked flounder Florentine topped off with apple pie a la mode. Connie had the same but she copped out on the apple pie and had grape nut pudding instead. Gabby's is one of those really old-fashioned places, a railroad dining car that has been added onto. George, the owner, specializes in good home cooking. He never put out a meal that wasn't satisfying. That was his motto: "My customers leave here satisfied or they don't leave at all." It was printed right there on the wall over the menu.

"What do you do with them when they don't leave?" asked Connie.

"So far I haven't had to worry about it," he said with a straight face.

Our waitress, Maria, dropped off the bill and said, "Word is you've had a busy day out on the dunes. I knew George and Jenny Willis. They used to come in here all the time. I think those men that killed them were here the other day. I told Sergeant Cronkite about them this morning. They were acting really funny, asking questions about you and your cottage. One of the customers told them where you lived."

"I hope you told John who that was," I said.

"Yeah, it was some truck driver from over Riverhead. It wasn't his fault. He was just trying to be helpful, you know?"

"Yeah, well, tell that to George and Jenny," I said.

I drove to the marina, opened the boat and we started stowing our gear below. It was a Concordia Yawl, in peak condition, one of the finest wooden boats ever built. It represented more than a means of recreation. It was a sanctuary from the world. Now it was the last place Connie and I could crash and catch a few Z's.

"Wake me when it's over, Bill," she said.

"Only if you promise to love me forever," I said and she promised.

It was nearing sunset when we came back to reality. My slumbers had been dominated by images of black clad terrorists floating down from the sky, shooting automatic weapons at me. One of them looked like Victor Cantrelli and another like his bodyguard. The leering face of John Delmar kept popping up everywhere I turned, and there was the sad-eyed expression of my son, Timothy, his hand raised, waving goodbye as I drove away. That's when I woke up. Connie sat on the opposite bunk in the main salon, looking at me, an expression of concern on her face.

"Hi, been awake long?" I asked.

"Awhile," she answered. "You had nightmares. Are you all right?"

"Yes, I guess so." I sat up, my body dripping wet with sweat. "Just had a few struggles to resolve while I was asleep."

"Like I said, nightmares," she said.

"Okay, okay, I had dreams, unpleasant dreams. Freud says that's how we release psychic tension. People who don't dream go insane."

"I can believe that." She hesitated. "Bill? What happened back there in the cottage? Why did Hank Gaines say that you lost it?"

"I don't know if I should tell you," I said, wiping my face with a towel.

"Please, don't treat me like a child. I'm in this all the way with you and I deserve to know what we're up against."

"All right, maybe you can make some sense out of it."

I told her everything about Alexander the Chicago police sergeant, Cantrelli, SARTXE, the phone numbers in the little black book, and last but not least, John Delmar. When I finished, she just sat there. Then she stood and slammed her fist into the bulkhead over the bunk. I never saw her get that physical before.

"Damn him, that John Delmar...President and General Manager of Daytime Inns, my boss, a man I trusted and respected, and he's part of it. He's SARTXE. Wait until I get my hooks into that slimy SOB. I'll kill him myself."

She turned to face me and said in a calm voice, "I can, you know. I used to help my dad slaughter pigs on the farm. I know just how to do it. That lousy Delmar low-life is connected to all this and he has the gall to act concerned over me. Yuk! He even put his arm around me." She whacked the bulkhead again. Her breathing was short and labored and she was sweating.

"Betrayal by those we trust is the worst hurt of all. John Delmar is a little fish, a second level peon who reports up the line. Whoever is at the top commands more authority and power than you can imagine. Think of it this way. Only the President of the United States can approve a strike by a squad of Navy Seals, so either the President is in on SARTXE, or SARTXE commands the same powers as the President."

"Bill, we should leave here and never come back. This is too big. We'll never beat them," she said and she began to cry.

I took her in my arms. "Not so, my sweet young damsel. Not to fear, O'Keefe is here. I've played this game before, and with even bigger odds. Every conspiracy has its lynch pin, its weak point, its cornerstone. This is my specialty and I don't scare easily.

"David and Goliath, right?" said Connie, shaking her head in disbelief and wiping the tears from her face.

"More like the Wizard of Oz. These people are only human and I'll prove it. They already made some very sloppy mistakes. They left a trail a blind man could follow right to the wicked witch of the west."

"That could be intentional. They may be trying to draw you out into a trap."

"That's possible, but if you're stalking the Tiger, you'd better be ready with a real good trap and a lot of heavy artillery when he comes to you. More than one great white hunter has been chewed up alive by the very tiger he was stalking."

"Yuck! You make it sound so simple."

"In the end it will be. We'll crack this thing and look back at it laughing because it will be so simple. You'll see."

"If you say so. Meanwhile I need a shower, a change of clothes, a light supper, and a heavy drink," she said.

"All of which can be had for only a small fee, my dear. I will rustle up something while you do the shower thing."

Connie took her duffle bag and went to the marina showers at the head of the docks. While she was gone, I wandered across the street to the Perkins General Store to pick up a few provisions. It was Saturday night and most of the boat people were out so things were slow. I was still dressed, that is to say I still had my Glock strapped on my left ankle but I left the .44 magnum in the boat.

Perkins was actually several stores, the result of a successful business venture, which required more space, so the original owner had expanded into the stores on either side in the same building. There were three entrances, one in the front and one on either side leading into small alleyways between buildings. The store was a cutup hodge-podge arrangement with steps up and down to the different levels of the previous stores. If that wasn't enough, there were several stairways going up to a second floor where the dry goods were displayed and Arnold Perkins, the owner, kept his office.

As I look back, I realize the layout of the store probably saved my life. Tonight Arnold Perkins was at home with his wife, Elsie. Their son, Gerry, was tending the store. There were two young girls buying sodas. They were more interested in Gerry than the soda, so I took my time: a quart of milk, some lemon cookies, a package of hot dogs - the mustard was already on board - two cans of beef stew, four cans of chili with beans, a loaf of Birnbaums Dark Rye, a half pound of sliced baked ham, a few slices of provolone, a jar of kosher dills, a head of lettuce, four small firm tomatoes, and a bag of ice. Everything else was stowed on board the boat and waiting.

I thought Connie would be waiting on board too, but I was wrong. Just as I stepped through the front door of the store, the middle one which Gerry had propped open for ventilation, right then as I was still half in and half out, that is to say one foot over the threshold, I saw Connie come out of the showers and start down the gangplank to the dock leading to the boats. I was planning to admire her as she walked the plank, so to speak, but a movement off to my right caught my attention. I looked that way and got a glimpse of two characters slithering along the parking lot fence to the entrance of the dock area to Connie's right. I noticed them because they were out of place. They were wearing dark suits, hats, shirts with ties and suede shoes. I remembered the shoes later.

The point is they just didn't fit and also there were the guns. Each one was carrying an M-16. There wasn't much time, but for some reason, I stopped just outside the door and set my groceries carefully on the sidewalk next to the front window of the store. When I looked back on it later, I could not for the life of me explain why I took the time to do that but I did. Then I stood up and yelled.

"Connie! Yo Connie! Over here." I waved at her.

She turned and I pointed to the two dudes with the M-16s slithering through the fence. I waved for her to come back when one of them cut loose at me with his gun. They were only a hundred feet away, but he didn't take time to aim. He just cut loose from the hip, John Wayne style. He missed me but he hit the front windows of Perkins General Store, sending fragments of shattered glass flying everywhere.

The other gunner joined in and the last thing I remember of Connie was seeing her go off the gangplank into the water. I didn't know if she had been hit or not because I was too busy cutting my hands and knees on the broken glass as I crawled back through the front door of the store. They must have run out of ammo because the firing stopped and Gerry came running to the front of the store. I grabbed his arm and pulled him down next to me behind a pile of potatoes in fifty pound bags stacked inside the front door.

"What's...what's goin' on, Mr. O'Keefe?"

"Terrorists, Gerry...freakin' terrorists. Get down."

I pulled my gun and rolled over for a peak out the door. They were coming across the street, M-16s at their hips. They started firing again, spraying bullets all over the place. These guys were real mashers and so were the potatoes. I rolled back, grabbed Gerry, and dragged him around the corner of the canned juice aisle, which by now was leaking a mixture of flavors all over the floor.

"Come on, Gerry. Let's get the hell out of here. Those are real bullets and we gotta get outta here now."

"Where are we going?" He just didn't get it so I dragged him along behind me.

The firing stopped again and I stood up, ran for the side door dragging Gerry behind, and plunged into the alley.

"Come on kid, we gotta set up a perimeter so we can draw these guys out." I checked the street and found it empty so I led the way across into the parking lot where I took up a position behind a line of Jersey barriers which separated the sidewalk from the marina parking lot.

"Gerry! You have to do as I say." His face was a blank. He was in shock. "You gotta stay down, flat on the ground. Do you understand?" He stared at me but he nodded.

I knew we didn't have much time before those two bozos realized I wasn't inside the many levels and corners of that store, and they would come out looking for me. People were starting to come out of the buildings lining the street. Behind me I could hear people calling from their boats. The whole area would soon become a killing field. I turned and saw someone running along the dock. It was Connie and she was headed across the street to the store thinking I was still there.

I stood and waved at her. She saw me after I called her name and she turned through the gate into the parking lot, soaking wet and out of breath but she was unharmed. I got her down safe behind the barriers and looked around. It was time to get organized.

CHAPTER SEVENTEEN

"OH, THANK GOD...BILL...YOU'RE ALIVE. I thought they got you." She had my duffle bag and she handed it to me with shaking hands.

"I brought your gun. I was going to shoot them, but now you can do it," she said, shaking all over.

She handed me the Ruger .44 Magnum and then a box of ammo. The gun was an old one but it was an awesome weapon and my favorite in a head to head firefight like this. Its kick has been known to break bones in a man's hand and sprain wrists and elbows. I checked the loads and looked over the barrier at the store. They were coming out of the front door. They couldn't see us so I decided to wait until they got closer. We were maybe seventy-five feet away, which is a fair shot for any handgun under the best of circumstances, but in a situation like this with people shooting at you, it's twice as hard to keep a steady hand. Just as I thought it might be working, Gerry stood up and started yelling.

"Help...Help...H...!"

"I grabbed him by his hair and slammed him to the ground but it was too late. Bullets were slapping into the concrete barriers, whizzing over our heads, and smashing into cars behind us in the parking lot. I tried to gauge the distance they were from our line of barriers by the sound of the gunfire. They were amateurs. Instead of alternating their fire so that one was firing while the other was reloading, they both just put it on automatic and pulled the trigger, from the hip of course.

"Keep him down," I yelled to Connie.

I crawled along to the next barrier and waited until they stopped. Then I stood up and commenced firing the Glock two-handed, aiming at their bodies, alternating right and left, three or four shots for each. I fired until the gun was empty. By then both men were down on their hands and knees, turned sideways to me about fifty feet away in the middle of the street. I knew something was wrong even before one of them stood up and aimed his rifle at me. I realized right then that they were wearing bulletproof vests. I hit the pavement just as the one on the right started firing again. It was close, and as the other one joined in I made the decision to finish this battle before anyone else got hurt.

I crawled past two more barriers to the right and waited. Their firing was intense. I waited until they stopped again, and I rolled up on my knees and cut loose with the .44 Magnum, using the Jersey barrier as a rest. I was to their left so I was firing at an angle and I aimed low to get under the vests: one shot at each man. I knew I would knock them down and I was right. The power of the .44 Magnum is unreal. The one on the right was out of it, no doubt about it. He was flat on his back and his left leg was about five feet away. He'd literally been blown in half. The other one was on his side twitching like a bolt of lightening had hit him.

I moved forward and kicked the rifles away from them. Each one had a handgun in a belt holster and I took those. The one on the left was terminal. The bullet had gone through the edge of the bulletproof vest, passed through his solar plexus and out through his back, smashing his spine. Both vests were riddled with the 9mm slugs from the Glock. One was wounded in the leg and the other in the arm, but I hadn't stopped either one with the first salvo from the Glock.

"Are...are they dead?" Connie asked.

She stood behind me, barefoot, soaked and shivering, her teeth chattering probably more from shock than anything else. I was hot and tired but I still had work to do. I checked the gunner on the left again and found he was dead. He had a brown envelope full of money inside his right suit coat pocket. His driver's license said he was Anthony Torleni from Brooklyn. The address meant nothing to me at the time. I put the license back in the wallet and stuffed the wallet in his back pants pocket but I kept the brown envelope.

The shooter on the right was still alive. He had a brown envelope too and he could talk. I didn't have to check his I.D. He was Victor Cantrelli's bodyguard who was supposed to have been shot and killed at the estate on July Fourth by the Latinos. Obviously he was very much alive and well until now.

"Who sent you?" I asked.

"Go stuff it, jerk." He didn't grasp the significance of the moment.

"You don't get it, do you? I shot you. That's your leg over there and you're bleeding all over the street. You're going to die, bambino. You're done so why don't you clear your conscience while you tell me who sent you?"

Reality began to dawn on him when he tried to move. The pain must have been excruciating but he didn't give in easily.

"Get me a priest...I want a priest."

"Forget it, slime. Talk to me or no priest. Die and go to hell."

"Okay, okay, I'll tell ya anything you want."

"Who sent you? Was it Victor Cantrelli?"

"No."

"Who, Damn it?" He hesitated and I thought he was gone.

"SARTXE." He said in a whisper.

"Is Cantrelli, SARTXE?" He shook his head, no.

"I watch Cantrelli. He does what they say and I watch him."

"Who is SARTXE?" He shook his head again.

"I don't know...a voice...a phone call."

"What's the number? Give it to me."

He tried to reach into his jacket pocket but his hand stopped halfway. I checked his inside suit coat pocket and found a black notebook just like the one the dead man at my cottage was carrying. I looked at his face, but I knew it was no use because he was gone. People were beginning to gather and I didn't need to answer any questions.

"Bill," said Connie. "Gerry Perkins is wounded." I walked over and checked him. He had taken one in the shoulder but it wasn't bleeding too much. Others were gathering and one man said he'd called for an ambulance.

I took Connie by the hand and walked her down to the boat, her teeth chattering all the way. While she changed into dry clothes, I picked glass slivers out of my hands and knees. Then I took a twelve-ounce brandy snifter, filled it half full with twelve year old Tennessee Sour Mash Whiskey and started going through the little black book.

I found the same addresses and phone numbers for SARTXE in Champaign, Illinois as Sergeant Vitro Alexander had in his book, but there was more. Victor Cantrelli's address and telephone numbers were listed for Albany, Brooklyn, and Washington, D.C. I found Jack Sullivan's number and address, and listings for Admiral Rassmussen, Ambassador Kitterage, and Salvatore Santiago; all the men who were at Jack's office after the robbery on the Fourth of July. But Victor Cantrelli couldn't be there because he had to go to the hospital with his bodyguard who was dying. Only he wasn't dying then, he died later, like tonight, and it was time to do something about all the lies and deceptions, all the violence and death these people were causing.

Victor Cantrelli was a big-cheese United States Senator, but he wasn't all that big in SARTXE, because he had a bodyguard who was watching him to make certain he did what he was supposed to. If Admiral Rassmussen, Ambassador Kitterage, and Salvatore Santiago were in SARTXE, then these were indeed very powerful enemies for the making. I had stumbled onto the mother nest.

Someone stepped on board the boat. "Ahoy there, O'Keefe? You down there, Buddy?" It was Tom Green, owner of the marina.

"Yeah, come aboard." I held the Glock in my right hand under a cushion, just in case, but Tom came down the ladder alone.

"Police want to talk to you." He eyed my hands and knees. "You all right, Man?" Connie came out of the head.

"We're all right, Tom, how about you?" I asked.

"Gerry Perkins took a bullet in the shoulder but you saved him. I guess he was lucky. Besides that, it's just a lot of broken glass and smashed potatoes. Damn, O'Keefe! I've heard about you. I was in the

Navy, but I never saw nothing like what you did up there tonight. I gotta tell ya, man, goin' head to teeth against two M-16s like that with nothin' but a handgun...why hell! It's just plain awesome."

"Thanks, Tom, couldn't have said it better myself. Look, I'll be up in a few minutes. I have to change and fix up these cuts."

"Okay, I'll tell them you're coming."

"Are you all right?" Connie sat down next to me.

"Sure, I'll be all right in a few minutes, Babe. It's just...the shaking. Always...the damn shakes," and the nausea which I didn't want to think about.

I sat there with Connie holding me for maybe ten minutes before they subsided. I washed and dressed my cut knees and changed into clean slacks and a shirt. I strapped the Glock back on my left ankle and the knife on my right. Nothing was over until the end, and this was only the beginning. I walked stiffly up the gangplank to the street where the police, paramedics, and firefighters were gathered with their flashing lights and sirens, each group competing with the other in self-importance to see who could make the most noise and flash the brightest lights. Some paramedics were loading Gerry Perkins into to an ambulance.

"You the guy that did all this?" A reporter stuck a microphone in my face. Without thinking I straight-armed him out of the way. He landed hard on his back, taking a cameraman down with him.

"Hey, wowwa...take it easy fella." A uniformed cop ran over and grabbed me by the arm. I looked him in the eyes and he let go, getting the message.

"Ahh, come this way please," he said. "The Chief wants to talk to you." He led the way.

I looked around at the faces in the crowd. Arnold Perkins was there, an anxious look on his face, his wife Elsie next to him. They were talking to some of their friends in the crowd. I went over and took Arnold's arm.

"Can I talk to you?"

"Yes...of course...ahh, say, thanks for taking care of my boy. I guess he sort of lost it. Are you okay, Mr. O'Keefe?" I was amazed at his concern for me. The Perkins were good people and they didn't deserve this.

"I'm fine." We walked into the store and I stopped behind the pile of smashed potato sacks where Gerry and I had crouched on the floor, and handed him the two brown envelopes.

"I am very sorry about all this. I don't know how much is there but maybe it will help. If anything is left over, there are people whose cars were damaged. I'll leave it up to you. I'm glad Gerry is safe and don't blame him. There is no amount of training that can prepare a man for being under fire, let alone a boy like Gerry. When you see him, tell him for me, it's okay. He did good and I'll be over to talk to him later. He did just fine."

"Thanks...I guess there's no way we can turn the clock back, Mr. O'Keefe, but I sure do wish this had never happened," said Arnold Perkins.

I left him and went in search of the Chief of Police. He was surrounded by reporters so I faded into the background until he was finished. He was a man in his sixties, stout but not fat, about 5'10", gray hair. He wore a white shirt with a nametag, which read "Charles Panetella" and a hat with gold braid. His face was flushed a deep red and his voice had a quiver in it. When I introduced myself, he just stood there and glared at me.

"You sure took your time showing up. You got a lot to answer for, mister. What do you think you're doin' here, playin' shoot out at the O.K. Corral? This is a peaceful town, not some Wild West show. Look, Mr. Whatever-your-name-is, if you're packin' a gun, I want it right now. I don't intend to have any more of this sort of thing goin' on in my town."

People were gathering around us, curious about the yelling, and some of them were reporters with tape recorders and cameras. I didn't need publicity at this point. So far I'd remained anonymous, so I took Chief Panetella by the arm and turned him toward the general store.

"Chief, why don't we take a little private walk so we can talk? Maybe your boys could keep these reporters away while I show you what happened."

He resisted at first, then he turned, waved two of his officers over and gave them instructions. He came back to me and we started walking across the street.

"So show me what happened, Mr. Shoot 'em up."

I told him about seeing the two shooters with the M-16s, and Connie going down the gangplank, the shooting, the glass, the bullets smashing through the potato sacks, my cut hands and knees, the juice aisle, the aroma of spilt juices permeating the air, and then the side door out into the alley. I gave him the flavor of what it was like standing in front of two M-16s going full out on automatic fire. He resisted my suggestion that he lay down on the floor and roll around like Gerry and I had done. Then I took him through the alley and across the street to the barriers.

"Did your men count the shell casings?"

"No! Why should they?"

"It might help you understand how intense the fire was and why Gerry Perkins panicked."

Then I explained the killing field theory and how innocent but curious people might have accidentally come under fire, and why I had to stop the two shooters before people started running into the street. I explained about the Glock 17 and the flak jackets and the .44 Magnum to impress upon him that I'd used the minimum amount of force to stop the attackers. I could see him slowly coming around. He was impressed but didn't want to admit it. Most police are not schooled in field tactics. Their situation training always assumes a group of police surrounding a criminal. They're not accustomed to massive terrorist attacks, but then, who is? By the time I finished explaining my stand at the barriers, Chief Panetella was very quiet and attentive.

"You have evidently done this before, Mr. O'Keefe," he said.

"Yes, more times than I care to remember. Look, Chief, I didn't go looking for this fight and I never thought they would try a dumb stunt like this. It was a suicide mission and they sent two bozos to do the job. I think you should contact the State Police and ask for Lieutenant Hank Gaines. He's already working on this case and he knows who the players are. Other than that, I suppose I'll be out of here tomorrow so you won't have to worry about another attack like this one."

"Funny you should mention Hank Gaines," said Panetella. "When we put this on the wire, he called in and said he was on his way, and he especially wanted to know if you and your lady friend were all right."

I promised to make a written statement for him in the morning and walked back to the Perkins General Store where my groceries still rested by the front door. They were completely undamaged except for some splinters of glass and wood. I picked them up and returned to the boat. Tom Green stopped me as I passed his office.

"Bill, I've been meaning to tell you something," he said. "There were three men in suits here July 4th looking for you. They wanted to go on board your boat but I wouldn't let them." He described them and the third one fit the description of Sergeant Vitro Alexander.

"It's a good thing you didn't let them near my boat. That last fellow you described killed Ginny Willis at my cottage a couple of hours after he left here. Hank Gaines will want to talk to you about the other two. They killed George Willis too."

"Oh no, the Willises are dead?" Tom said, shaking his head.

"Yes, we found them this morning. Sorry Tom, we all liked George and Ginny. Someone is trying to kill me and they don't care who gets hurt. I'm sorry."

I left Tom with his thoughts and went back to the boat. Connie was waiting for me in the cockpit, combing her long auburn hair. She'd changed into a pair of shorts and one of my T-shirts, no bra. The woman was enticing. I filled her in on what happened and we ate some crackers and cheese followed by a can of warmed over beef stew and a bottle of rose´ wine. When the wine was gone she went below, and after a few minutes she called me.

"Bill? Could you come here, please?"

I went below and found her there in the lamp light of the main cabin, standing stark naked, wearing only a smile on her face.

"What's a damsel in distress have to do to get a sailor to make love to her around here?"

"Well, first of all, we have to search the ship to see if there are any able and willing sailors aboard to do the job."

"Well, get on with it, Captain," she said.

So, I did.

CHAPTER EIGHTEEN

I AWOKE OUT OF A sound sleep not really sure where I was. The light of the gimbaled lamp glowed dimly in the dark and I decided to turn it up. My legs were stiff, my knees hurt, my hands throbbed, and I had a pounding headache from the wine and the evening's activities. Then again, maybe I was getting too old for the game of shoot 'em up. I stretched my stiff muscles, scratched, sat up, banged my head on the upper bunk, took a step toward the head, caught my foot on an open locker drawer, and fell flat on my face.

Connie, who was curled up on the port side bunk, shifted her hips, murmured something, and went back to counting sheep. I pulled my head out of a pile of sail bags and set about untangling my foot from the drawer while trying to find 'up' from 'down'. I got the urge for a walk after going to the head, so I put on a pair of shorts, a shirt, and sandals. I adjusted the gimbaled lamp and as an afterthought, I took the Glock and stuck it in my waist under the shirt. The clock on the bulkhead read midnight as I came on deck. The night was warm and a cool moist easterly brushed across my face as I climbed the plank to dry land and headed for the office. The moon peeked out occasionally from behind a broken overcast, giving an indication of what the dawn would bring. My spirits matched the generally overcast nature of the night.

On an impulse, I picked up the pay phone on the outside wall of the marina office and dialed the number of the Sullivan estate, being certain to add my credit card number. It rang twice before Corsini answered.

"Agent Corsini," he said. That was how I knew who it was.

"Corsini, this is O'Keefe. How's it going up there?"

"Pretty quiet this end. How's it with you?"

"About the same. I was just thinking about the kids and wondered how they are."

"Why don't you ask them yourself? They're right here. Every time the phone rings they run to see who it is."

We talked for maybe an hour. Samantha said she missed me and how was Connie? Jonathan wanted to go sailing and Timothy wanted to know when he would see me again. I promised soon and went back to Corsini.

"Things have been sort of dicey out this way," I said. "You may want to tighten up security there."

"Yeah, we had a watch on you and it reads like a Dirty Harry movie. We're ready here if anyone tries something." "You better be. We're not dealing with terrorists but they use the same tactics."

"I gotta tell ya, O'Keefe. That terrorist thing came straight from Washington. The Director himself said to treat the whole situation as a one time terrorist attack and not to get too serious. I have a different idea about it now."

"Did he say where his orders came from?"

"He wouldn't say exactly but he indicated he had White House authorization. I asked if it was the President and he said it was close. This is off the record so don't go quoting me. I'm telling you because you're the one they're shooting at."

"Thanks, I owe you. Keep looking over your shoulder and don't trust anyone."

"Don't worry about me, O'Keefe," and he hung up. Well, hell, I warned him didn't I?

It was beginning to spit rain. There were no more breaks in the clouds, no moon peeking out, and no nice warm sunny days coming up. An ill wind was coming and it would rain and storm. I picked up the phone, dialed Chicago and woke up Jack Chusak.

"Man, don't you ever sleep? Do you know what time it is here? It's after midnight."

"If I knew what time it was in Chicago, I wouldn't have to call you to find out what time it is. I get confused with this daylight savings stuff, so I have to call you to get a straight answer."

"You are crazy, O'Keefe."

"No, Jack, I am not crazy but I wish I was."

I told him about the murders at my cottage and Sergeant Vitro Alexander, the dead Chicago cop who killed Ginny Willis. I gave him the SARTXE address and telephone number in Champaign. I told him about John Delmar and the connection to Cantrelli, and waited until he stopped swearing and threatening to, "...strangle the SOB." When he was through and had calmed down, he reported on the names I'd given him.

"Senator Victor Cantrelli was a Navy Seal. He came out of the service and went into the real estate business with his cousin, Anthony Pinucci. They made a bundle although there's some question where all the money came from. Pinucci went on to head Jersey Mutual Insurance while Cantrelli moved up country to Troy and ran for the U.S. Senate. Needless to say, he spent a lot of money and blew the local favorite off the face of the earth."

"Was Cantrelli ever involved in Jersey Mutual with Pinucci?"

"Yes, as a matter of fact he was, but when he ran for the Senate he put all his visible holdings in a blind trust and his name was dropped from the board of directors of the company. He wanted to appear clean. Some of his earlier deals were pretty shady, like filling in marshlands using state owned trucks and gravel. He almost got nailed on that one but some key witnesses suddenly died and others left the country."

"So Cantrelli was a Navy Seal, involved in Jersey Mutual and he's connected with SARTXE. I would bet he was also involved with the robbery at the Sullivan's in some way," I said.

"He has three places of operation: one in Brooklyn and one in Rensselaer near Albany, then one in Georgetown which is his Washington, D.C. address."

John told me he was working on the other names and would get back to me. I hung up the phone and turned to find a uniformed policeman standing a few yards away.

"Hello, officer," I said.

"Good morning, sir. Is everything all right?"

"Yes, of course. I was just calling some friends, why?"

"Chief said to keep an eye on you...I mean on things. He said not to let anything more go wrong here."

"I'm glad to hear that. Maybe now I can sleep." I returned to my bunk and fell asleep immediately.

I woke to the gentle sound of rain falling on the cabin roof in the morning. Connie had bacon and eggs, biscuits with honey and a hot coffee chaser when I finally rolled out of my bunk and sat up. I was careful not to bump my head or trip over anything.

"What are you doing, Bill?"

"Counting my body parts, Babe."

"It's all there, Tiger. I already checked."

"So, it wasn't just a dream. Was I good?"

"Terrific as usual, but if you don't remember, I'll do it again right after breakfast."

"Nympho!" I tried to stand up, stretching through the pain.

"You should be so lucky," she said flipping an egg.

We were cleaning dishes when Hank Gaines came to the main hatch and called down.

"You folks decent? I'm coming down."

"Welcome aboard, Hank."

"Boy oh boy what a great day for ducks."

"Have some coffee. There are some biscuits and honey still left over." I poured him a cup of steaming hot coffee.

"Thanks, don't mind if I do. Man, what's goin' on with you, O'Keefe? They say you stood down two shooters with M-16s and took them out with just two shots. Damn! Wish I'd seen that. I never get to see the action any more."

"Not that big a deal, Hank. They were bozos, jerks with big ideas. They came straight on, triggers down. They didn't even alternate or fire in bursts. I waited for them to run out of ammo and while they were reloading I popped up and had at them. Trouble was they wore bulletproof vests and after I unloaded the Glock, they just got back up and kept coming. So, I waited for them to run out again and I took them out with the .44 Magnum. That went through everything. I was lucky but this can't keep up much longer."

"I don't know, man. It sounds like a real high to me. You know how long it's been since I saw action?" He shoved a whole biscuit in his mouth and chomped on it.

"It's not all that much fun, Hank. It never was you know."

"It's the adrenaline rush, the high is unreal. I haven't had anything like it since Nam. You know what I do? I come in when it's all over and sweep up the mess. I never get in on any of the action. I'm just a damn janitor who sweeps up the bodies. I'm goin' to retire in three years and then it'll be all over for me. Geeze, I envy you, O'Keefe. You got the life, man."

"You're making me blush, Hank. I know how you feel but too many innocent people get hurt when these jerks show up with automatic weapons and start shooting everything in sight."

"I think I know what Hank is trying to say." Connie said, buttering another biscuit and handing it to him. "He's saying that your life has meaning, Bill, while his is dull and routine."

"Yeah! You said it, Connie. That's what I was trying to say but old bonehead here wouldn't let me get it out."

"You can get it out any time, friend," I said, "just leave me that last biscuit."

"No way man. Buddies we may be, but not where biscuits and honey are concerned. By the way, that fellow we found dead in your cottage, Sergeant Vitro Alexander, he's a very bad boy. He was not supposed to be here on Long Island. I talked to his Chief and he says Sergeant Vitro was supposed to report to work on July 5th. They're checking to find out who else was with him."

"Did they check airport security cameras?"

"The chief was genuinely shocked and he promised to check that as well as reservations; who sat with who, and all that stuff."

"Sounds like there's going to be a lot of heat in Chicago."

"Yeah, but not as much as there's gonna be right here because the guy you popped last night, the one who lost the leg, is connected, no pun intended. He's Senator Cantrelli's personal bodyguard."

"I know that. He was supposed to have been shot and mortally wounded in the robbery attempt at Jack Sullivan's estate on July 4th.

It was a smoke screen to make it look like Cantrelli had nothing to do with the robbery. It also provided a very convenient reason for him to leave and go to the hospital."

"Yeah, well this bodyguard is Salvatore Pinucci, brother of Anthony Pinucci, President and CEO of Jersey Mutual, who was once partners with Victor Cantrelli in some pretty shady real estate deals. This implicates Victor Cantrelli for real," said Hank.

"Wait a minute. Let me get this straight. You just said that guy who lost a leg is related to Anthony Pinucci? That's his brother?" I was stunned. I neglected to check his I.D. and that was a mistake.

"Yeah," said Hank. "Why?"

"Hank, Anthony Pinucci owes a lot of money to somebody that I'm working for. If Victor Cantrelli is tied to that, then it makes this case one big ball of wax. Everything is related."

"Yeah, well, that's your business. I still gotta go see Cantrelli."

"You may want to take this with you." I handed him the black address book I took off the dead Pinucci the night before. "It matches the one you got off that dead sergeant yesterday at my place."

"You sure opened a can of worms," said Hank.

"Maybe you should take someone from the State Attorney General's office to do the actual questioning and transfer the heat upstairs where it really belongs. Cantrelli isn't that popular up in Albany. His base of support is in Brooklyn plus what votes he can buy upstate with his money and dirty tricks. There are probably plenty of people who would like to see him brought down. Sal Pinucci told me last night, while he was dying, that his job was to watch Cantrelli for SARTXE to make sure he did what he was supposed to do. So, Cantrelli may not be as important as he thinks."

"I'd rather face two M-16s on full auto than talk to Victor Cantrelli, but maybe you're right. Let the politicians handle it, right? I'll talk to my Captain and let him take the credit. I've had enough of this kind of fame to last me a lifetime."

I told Hank about Tom Green and the three visitors to the marina on July 4th and my conversation with Jack Chusak the previous night. He promised to check back as soon as he had anything new and he left, taking the last honey-soaked biscuit with him. "One for the road," he said and he waved goodbye.

So, Salvatore Pinucci was Anthony Pinucci's brother. Anthony was Victor Cantrelli's partner and the President and CEO of Jersey Mutual where Jack Sullivan's money disappeared. The puzzle was starting to take shape. It was time to go on the offensive, but first there was an after breakfast promise to collect from a damsel in distress.

CHAPTER NINETEEN

MY INTENTIONS WERE TO sail away with Connie for a short vacation while the craziness of the last few days dissipated, but the rain was heavy and forecast to last for the next two days. Sailing is fun when done correctly and that means when you are well rested, dry, well fed, warm, and feeling good all over.

"You sound like an old salty dog," said Connie, looking at her hair in the mirror.

"Sailing is no joke," I said. "What if we were going flying instead of sailing? Would you not want your pilot to be well rested, with good eyesight, and his mind on his job? You don't want to hear he had no sleep for three days, his business was failing, he had five Manhattans for lunch, his girlfriend has a communicable disease, and his wife just left him. Then he pops a beer as he's taxiing out for takeoff. That's the condition of many recreational sailors when they depart the docks and head out for a day on the bay."

"But isn't flying more dangerous?" Connie said as she put on a pair of pink shorts.

"Maybe death comes at a greater speed in flying, but more people are injured and killed in boating accidents each year than in aircraft mishaps."

"If that's so, then why don't they do something about it?" She said, buttoning her shirt.

"Who's they? The Coast Guard gives courses, does inspections, makes arrests, and tries to help anyone in need. The Power Squadron and Coast Guard Auxiliary provide courses to the public and help with any emergency they encounter. Yacht clubs and sailing clubs work for boating safety and education, yet the accidents continue."

"So what's the problem?" Connie was brushing her hair.

"It's the Joe-Shmoe-bozo who thinks going out on the water provides him with a license to commit mayhem, the uneducated know-it-all public that doesn't care about anyone else. They buy a hot rocket of a boat and hit the water drunk, ready to blow away anyone who gets near them. You see them wrecked up on top of the local breakwater, or aground in the flats out of the channel, because they don't know a channel marker from a beer can and couldn't read a chart if they had one."

"But doesn't someone watch these people?" She said bending over putting on her sandals.

"You see the ads on TV and in the newspapers. They say, 'Come on down and buy a boat or an RV or a two week time-share in a condo in Guatemala. This nifty little twenty-four footer comes equipped with two, two hundred-fifty horsepower inboard-outboard engines, a main salon that seats twenty-four relatives, and a forward bunk complete with two blonds, a brunette and a mermaid. Built in bar is standard, trailer comes with the boat, tires and tail lights are extra. Get the whole package, all for $129.99/month for the rest of your life. This is Sam Slime serving your boating needs.' "

"So, Frank and Judy trade in their collapsible trailer for a speed boat that will do 40 mph on a calm day and he goes out, scares hell out of his neighbors, his wife, the kids, himself, and half the boating public. If he lives, he takes the thing home, his wife refuses to go out with him again, so he plops it down in the front yard, and puts a 'For Sale' sign on it. It should be an automatic jail sentence for any salesman to let a person like that buy such a dangerous piece of machinery."

"I've never seen this side of you before. What's going on?" Connie said, as she tucked her shirt into her shorts.

"I suppose it's after shock. Here we are talking about boating safety in a world where hoodlums, terrorists, and Navy Seals are trying to kill us, and it seems like nobody really cares. I get the feeling we're two normal people, living in a totally insane world. The only thing that brings me back to reality is to watch you dress. It sort of makes everything else fade away," I said.

"Voyeur? I never thought you were the type," she said.

"Only where you're concerned," I replied.

"I'm feeling the same way but I know we're right in what we believe," Connie said. "If these big and powerful people are allowed to continue lying, stealing, and killing, there will be no sanity left. Unfortunately, it's you who has the key to stopping SARTXE. Somehow, someplace, somewhere, in your past, you know the answer. They wouldn't be after you…make that us…they wouldn't be after us if we weren't such a threat to them. It can't just be the money they lost in East Harbour, it has to be more. Somehow, you have uncovered something in SARTXE and they are determined to have you out of the way."

Connie's words struck me like a bolt of lightening. She made more sense than she realized.

"You're right, the East Harbour case was last September. Now it's July, ten months later. What suddenly caused them to come after me like this?"

"John Stanley, your old boss in State Mutual, said you really hurt them and they would get even," she said.

"I remember. We were visiting Willie Monk at the nursing home and I insulted John over the phone."

"You told him to stop sending amateurs after you. That you were tired and bored of dealing with them," Connie added.

"Well, he sure sent some pros this time but why did he wait ten months? Something must have happened recently. I haven't done any really big cases since East Harbour. I haven't shot anyone, taken anyone's money, or kissed anybody's wife or daughter."

"I should hope not." Connie punched me in the arm. "But what is the one big deal that has come up lately?" she asked.

"Jack Sullivan and his secret papers, but I didn't know anything about that until the robbery. The guys from Chicago were here on July 4th and your apartment was hit early on the fifth."

"Think about it," Connie said. "Those things took time to plan. No one expected you to be at the Sullivan's estate. You've been estranged from Natalie for years and you haven't been part of the family celebrations since the divorce, so anyone who knew your routines would just naturally assume you would be on your boat or with me for the holidays. Even John Delmar assumed we were in my apartment because your car was outside the building. The Navy Seals must have been ready to strike if Sergeant What's His Name, Vitro Alexander, from Chicago and his friends didn't succeed. Let's face it, they went where your car was," Connie said.

"You've put your finger on the problem that's been bothering me. The timing was all wrong. The attempted hit at the cottage was on the morning of July Fourth, but I showed up at the Sullivan's estate instead and caused a lot of damage. No one could have known we would stay at the estate. So, Delmar checked the parking lot late on July Fourth and saw my Caddy. He assumed we were in your apartment, and the Navy Seals were sent in. Then we show up alive and Delmar reports that we've left for Long Island. There were too many police at the cottage so they waited until we got here at the marina, and that's when Salvatore Pinucci and his pal, Anthony Torleni, showed up with the M-16s and pulverized Perkins General Store. They probably won't try again soon, at least not a frontal attack like before, not with the local police on patrol. Hank Gaines has the cottage under surveillance and your apartment is unlivable, so it's temporarily a stalemate."

"So, William, where do we go from here?" Connie said, grinning at me.

"I told ya a thousand times, woman, don't never use dat tone of voice wid me again. Ya hear me?" I mimicked my tough guy act and punched her lightly on the arm.

"I knew that would get your goat. That's why Judith calls you that. It's her way of putting you down."

"Yes, and speaking of the Sullivans, what time is it in Spain? I need to call Jack Sullivan."

"I have no idea. It must be earlier there."

"Not really. The earth is always turning toward the morning so it's later in Spain because it was morning there earlier than here."

"Now I'm really confused. Why do you want to call Jack?"

"You've put your finger on the motive for these attacks, and I want to find out if it's what I think it is."

I went to the office pay phone, called the overseas operator and received a thirty-minute delay. Fifteen minutes later the pay phone on the marina wall rang. I knew it was the overseas operator because of the two short rings, a pause, and two more short rings. I answered it and found Jack on the line.

"Billy, how are you? Is everything all right? How are the children?"

"Everything is okay, Jack. I just need to check with you on some details."

"All right, fire at will." I wished he wouldn't say that.

"I need to know if you mentioned my name to anyone before the July Fourth picnic at your house." There was a silence on the line and I thought we might have been disconnected.

"Jack...Jack? Are you still there?"

"Yes...I'm here. I did mention your name to a couple of people. One was Anthony Pinucci. I'm really sorry, but I was so upset I just lost it...I...ahh...I sort of, well…I threatened him. I told him I'd send you after him if he didn't give me my money back."

"What did he say?"

"He...ahh...it's so embarrassing...he just laughed and said not to insult him, that one man against a whole army was no contest. I'm really sorry if I caused you any problems. I was just so angry, I could have killed him for what he did."

"Okay, Jack, take it easy. Now think, did you talk to anyone else, anyone at all?"

"Well...yes, I told the committee, you know, the men you met in my office. I wanted them to meet you personally so they would have the same high opinion of you that I have. I wanted them to hire you to help us with the plan, you know, the one I told you about, the papers the terrorists stole out of my safe."

"When was that? When did you first talk to them and exactly who was there?"

"Well, it was, let me think...June, ahh...June 25th, a Tuesday. Yes, we had a meeting in New York City at Kitterage's place on upper Fifth Avenue. Let me think. Malcome Kitterage, the ambassador, was there of course. Admiral Rassmussen, Senator Cantrelli, Salvatore Santiago from the World Bank, they were all there. Also, there was someone else, but I'm not at liberty to mention his name."

"Jack! This is no time to be coy. There have been three attempts to kill me in the last three days. Last night Salvatore Pinucci and another hood tried to kill me with automatic rifles. Do you know who Salvatore Pinucci is, Jack?" I yelled. "He is Anthony Pinucci's brother, Jack, and Victor Cantrelli's personal bodyguard." There was total silence on the line. "Now tell me, damn it, who was the mystery guest at the damned meeting?"

"Oh God! No! It can't be!" Jack said, his voice breaking.

"Who was it, Jack? Tell me now or I'll personally go beat it out of Ambassador freakin' Malcome Kitterage."

"No ... No, that won't be necessary. It was...Oh no...I'll be hung for this. It was Samuel Sontaigm."

"The President's advisor?"

"Yes, but I'm certain he had nothing to do with it. Geeze, he's the President's advisor. He represented the President of the United States at that meeting. It's as if the President himself was there and spoke to us personally."

"Jack, have you ever actually spoken to the President or do you always speak to this Samuel Sontaigm when you call?"

"Well, yes, I am instructed to talk to Sontaigm. The President is a very busy man but we're friends, Bill. We go way back before he was ever elected to the U.S. Senate. We were school buddies."

"But when was the last time you actually spoke to him?"

"Let me think. It was some time in March. He called me. The phone rang in my office and I answered it, and the man on the other end said, 'Please stand by for the President of the United States'. He came on the line and told me about the plan and how he wanted me to head it up. Then he handed me over to Sontaigm and I've been talking to him ever since, but it's all the same. The President said that his advisors speak for him."

"Jack, think carefully now. Do you know what SARTXE means?" I spelled it out for him.

"No, never heard of it. Sounds like a chemical company, why?"

"Do you trust the President? Is he clean?"

"Absolutely! Damn it, Bill! You have no right. What do you think you're doing?"

"How about saving your measurable life and your fortune for

starters. The President may be clean, but I'll bet this Sontaigm is dirty. Trust me, and for your own sake, don't mention my name to any more of your friends or associates. I'm running out of ammunition and places to stay."

Jack cooled off and apologized and we talked awhile longer. I told him about my midnight telephone call to the kids and how I warned Corsini to tighten security. Jack said he ran with the bulls for about a hundred feet and all went well. He would go again tomorrow. I admired the old boy's spirit and I told him so. He laughed and we said goodbye.

It was raining steadily now and I was soaking wet, so what the heck, I just walked over to the shower house and took a long hot shower. I went to the boat dripping wet and toweled down in the main salon. Connie was puttering around in the galley so I gave her a kiss and a whack on the backside to let her know I still loved her and went to change.

There were decisions to be made and some of them involved people very near and dear to me. Next to the children, Connie was my number one concern. Then there was Willie Monk, my old partner and friend, the man who taught me what I know about the insurance business. Willie was in the South Fork Nursing Home but I didn't think anyone would try to get at him there. I was their target.

So, things were coming together. SARTXE had hatched a plan to steal the drug lord's money but they needed the backing of the President to bless it. The President called Jack Sullivan and Jack told them about me and they had to stop the plan from getting into the wrong hands. They were right to scared of me. I was their worst nightmare and it was far from over.

One thing we learned in Viet Nam was not to let the enemy rest no matter what the circumstances. It was time to go on the offensive. If they thought they'd been stung before, they would be surprised at what was coming at them now. The high and powerful lords of SARTXE sat in judgment in their boardrooms and back rooms. I would launch an archaeological expedition and dig around until I found the cornerstone that SARTXE was built on and then I would pull it out from under them and watch the whole thing come tumbling down.

So I presented my thoughts to Connie, who was through puttering about in the galley and was now putting out a scrumptious lunch of sautéed chicken breast smothered in mushrooms, peppers, onions and a touch of garlic; with mushroom gravy, candied baby carrots, wild rice, and a light blush pinot to finish it all off. Lady's got real class and she does it all.

CHAPTER TWENTY

WE CLEANED UP AFTER lunch, closed the boat, and headed for New York City. Traffic was light until we reached Forrest Hills, where we ran into some early commuters. I took the Queens Midtown Tunnel and headed downtown to the financial district. Driving into Manhattan is pure frustration and trying to find a parking place is sheer suicide, but I had an edge that most people can only dream about. I picked up the cell phone and dialed a number. It rang once and a sexy female voice answered.

"President's office."

"Kate, O'Keefe here."

"Oh my word, William, is that really you? Where are you?"

"I'm three blocks south on Broadway, coming in."

"I'll be waiting, lover boy. Just punch the button."

I drove three blocks, took a left, a right, and turned into a restricted entrance to the CIC building. I had done some work for Consolidated Insurance Companies in the past and they were always glad to see me any time I was in the city. Walter St. Onge was president and Kate Mulligan, his private secretary, was a very special and unusual lady. They weren't married but they should have been. I parked the Caddy and we took the elevator up to the fortieth floor. Kate was waiting for us as the door opened.

"William Thackery O'Keefe, you are a sight for sore eyes and who might I ask is this?" She gave Connie a thorough once over.

Kate was in her early thirties but she looked much younger. I made the introductions and we followed her to the president's office. She was a pert five feet tall, nicely built with long brown hair. I could easily have fallen in love with her but she chose one of my best friends instead.

He was no ordinary friend. I met him in Viet Nam but we weren't on the same team or even in the same outfit. Walter St. Onge was a Major on the General's Staff assigned to oversee the intelligence interface between the U.S. and South Vietnamese forces. He was a genius with languages and he had a capacity for details, which he compiled, analyzed, and stored in the central computer facilities at Headquarters Command. Eventually, he was the only one who could unravel the computerized information. That made him a target for the North Vietnamese and one night they kidnapped him. That's when we met.

My unit was Special Forces, designed for quick response missions into enemy territory. St. Onge was an army major but he was not a tough fighting type. He was an aristocrat, an MIT graduate who was promoted for his brains, and he should never have been left unprotected. The brass was afraid he wouldn't last long under interrogation, and what he knew was enough to damage our cause beyond repair. He was spotted under guard headed north. We were dropped into the area and spent a week playing tag with his captors before we caught up with them. He was in a North Vietnamese prison camp by then, under interrogation, and we were ordered to terminate him.

The squad took a vote to go in and get him out. It wasn't heroics. It was just plain anger at the stupidity of the brass. We left more than two-dozen prison guards and a Russian interrogator dead, and came away with Major St. Onge in tow. For our efforts we got a court martial because we exceeded orders. It was dropped only after my CO threatened to expose the stupidity of the brass. We were considered a rogue outfit, barely tolerated but needed, so the threat was taken seriously.

Walter St. Onge was a man who didn't age. He was still very fit, all 5'6" of him. His fine blond hair hung straight over his ears, giving him that little Dutch Boy appearance that often fooled his adversaries in the insurance and financial business. His family's money got him started but the rest, including the CIC building, were his own accomplishments. He was on the phone when we came in and he waved us to a seat. I stood when he hung up the phone and he came around the desk and threw his arms around me. There are friends and then there are friends who are buddies. Walter took Connie's hand and kissed it when I introduced her.

"Watch it, Lockenvar," Kate chided.

"Not to worry, lady," he said. "You're still my first love."

The view from his office over the financial district to the south was spectacular. We chatted for a while and caught up on the personal stuff and then I told Walter about the attacks beginning with the Fourth of July.

"I heard rumblings the past week and I wondered what was going on" Walter said. "This morning a claim came through the wires from Jersey Mutual for a policy on Pinucci, Salvatore, for one million dollars. At first I thought it was Anthony but then I realized it was his brother. Cause of death was listed as loss of blood, re: gun shot. One thing led to another and a few discrete inquiries turned up your name. So tell me what is this all about, Billy?"

"You know anything about SARTXE, Walter?"

He frowned, thought a moment and said, "Yes, I do. Some big names there and very hush, hush, why?"

"That's what's going on," I said.

He thought some more. "But why? Oh, now wait a minute! I'm not involved in SARTXE. I have nothing to do with them."

"I never believed you did, but I need your help, and if anyone can come up with something on SARTXE, you can."

"Okay, yes..." He was flustered for a moment. "Let me think. Yes... Anthony Pinucci approached me a few years ago. He and some others in the insurance business were building a network of very highly placed individuals, 'for the purpose of developing funds', that's what he said, 'developing funds', the use of which was strictly confidential. They decided I would be a good man to add to their roster. I told him no, flat out, No!"

"I've seen those kickback schemes before but never on such a high level and for such big bucks," he continued. "They call them origination fees, points, consulting fees, whatever you want, but I just don't want to get involved, especially with Anthony Pinucci. Besides, the only reason they asked me was because my computer services company down on the twentieth floor is on line with every insurance company and bank in the world. I don't sell or buy insurance, nor do I run a bank. I provide services for companies that do these things and if word got out, even so much as a whisper, that I was handling payoffs or kickbacks of any kind, no legitimate company would ever deal with me again."

"What is it you actually do?" Connie asked.

"It's complex," said Walter. "Simply put, part of my business is to provide wire services for other companies. Let us say a company like Aramco Oil needs bonding on a shipment of Arabian crude out of Abu Dhabi to New Orleans. Now, Aramco has lines, agents, facilities, and all that stuff but they don't usually deal in Abu Dhabi. They work out of Kuwait most of the time. Believe it or not, the lines of communication between Kuwait City and Abu Dhabi are in bad shape. They never were very good. Even a camel caravan could get a message through between many of the cities in the Middle East faster than a telex or any other form of communication. The problem is cultural, not electronic. Those people don't get along with each other, so they come to me. I can offer secure telex communications and banking services between all these ports of call and between my company and most banks. I'm faster and cheaper than the Central Telex and Banking facilities, which deal only between major worldwide banking institutions. You want to buy wool from the Falklands? I have agents and financial capabilities established all over the world. You need a letter of credit? I can help you."

"It sounds very complicated," said Connie.

"Not really," said Kate. "Don't let him snow you. The transfer of money doesn't occur as many people think. For instance, if you send a check by mail to your cousin in France and he cashes it, that's not really a transfer of funds. The actual transfer occurs when your check is confirmed by wire between the banks involved. If the money is not available in your account, the check bounces, no transfer of funds has occurred, and your cousin is out of luck."

"I can see now why SARTXE wants into your operation. It would make their scam a lot easier," said Connie.

"Yes," Walter agreed, "they would love the capability I have to be on line with so many financial institutions. That's why I have so much security around here. Did you know that Bill and his partner, Willie Monk, helped me set up the security arrangements in this building?"

"I'm not surprised. Actually, nothing surprises me any more since I met Bill."

"That's good," said Kate. "Keep an open mind. These two guys are always cooking up something new."

"So, O'Keefe," said Walter, "what's the operation?"

"SARTXE is trying to kill me."

"Let me guess, the East Harbor fiasco. You hurt them pretty bad."

"Yes, but there's something more in the stew. It goes all the way to the White House, and my ex-father-in-law is involved."

I told him the story, and when I finished he just stared out the large picture windows of his office at the rain soaked panorama of Manhattan. Then he slowly turned and started talking.

"Samuel Sontaigm is a wolf dressed in sheep's clothing. He was a stockbroker and then a banker here in New York City. Then he went to Chicago. I'm surprised you didn't know him when you worked for State Mutual under John Stanley. Sontaigm was John's inside trading broker. That's how Stanley made so much money and bought his way into the upper management of State Mutual out in Omaha. Another thing you should know is that Sontaigm was in the Navy Seals and he knew James Rassmussen before he became an Admiral.

Salvatore Santiago is another story. His family was in on the multi-million dollar loan scam from the World Bank to Brazil to build a railroad and develop the mineral wealth of the interior of the country. Thousands of settlers flocked to the area and staked land claims, which required them to clear the land. Most failed and many died. Santiago, who worked out of the Banco de Brazil, took part of the money at no interest and bought up the settlers' homesteads for next to peanuts. Then he and his friends ran the settlers off their mines and stole their claims. Now his family runs one of the biggest cattle ranches in the world along with silver and gold mines. The Banco de Brazil forgave him the loan, the World Bank forgave the Banco de Brazil, everybody got paid off, and Santiago is one of the richest dudes in South America."

"Good grief, what a scam," said Connie.

"What about Ambassador Kitterage?" I asked.

"He's the ambassador to the United Nations. The World Bank Group is actually the International Bank for Reconstruction and Development and provides developing countries with long-term loans. What better place to coordinate such an effort than the United Nations?"

"Do you think the President of the United States is in on this?" I asked.

"No way. He's too straight to risk involvement in SARTXE, but the project you described with Jack Sullivan heading it up may be a smoke screen," said Walter. "I'll bet that report is bogus and the President's very close friend and advisor, Samuel Sontaigm, probably altered it as well as the President's notes and signature. If it ever surfaced that the President of the United States was involved in a scheme to pilfer money, even illegal drug monies, from crooked banks and drug cartels, even that sort of money, the people of this country and throughout the world would lynch him. His life wouldn't be worth a pound of cow manure. You know, not all countries have such a strict viewpoint of life as we do here in America. In many countries, insider trading and special influence, not to mention drug trafficking, is considered a way of life."

"So you think SARTXE is Sontaigm and Jack Sullivan was a mistake?" I asked.

"Absolutely. Sontaigm probably sold some variation of the plan to the President, who jumped the gun by calling Jack Sullivan who mentioned you to his friends and they panicked. You're the last man they would want to let in on what they are doing. SARTXE probably does plan to loot the banks and drug cartels, but they don't need you or Jack Sullivan to do it. Good grief, O'Keefe, if they're successful, they will be the most powerful financial force in the world. They will own us all."

"Jack said they knew how to do it, Walter. What do you think he meant? After all, you said it, they would have to have an operation like yours to do it and that takes time to set up."

"There is no other operation like mine, anywhere, not any place in the whole world. I'm unique."

"Precisely!" I said. "They need your company."

"Oh, no! Don't say that. They wouldn't dare," Kate said.

CHAPTER TWENTY-ONE

DAYLIGHT WAS FADING AS the clouds settled lower, obscuring the taller buildings of the rain soaked city. We continued talking, exploring, studying possibilities, and fashioning a plan of action. Kate took Connie for a tour of the building and some woman talk, while Walter and I ran some preliminary tests. Walter had several computer terminals in his office, each associated with his different companies. That was Willie Monk's idea: separate the computer systems into smaller units instead of one big, more economical system.

"If you feed all the data to one terminal, you'll be more vulnerable to theft. I would love to find all the secrets of six different companies fed into one terminal if I was a corporate thief," Walter explained. All the terminals had anti-theft devices, most of which I didn't understand. In addition, there was a secret high speed printer dump in a closet behind the corner bar of the office which recorded all the transactions of the day, even those that an operator deleted or inserted with windows to drop the transaction out of the system. Another safety precaution provided by Willie Monk. It was considered out of date in today's modern high tech world but Walter kept it anyway.

"We caught a spy sending information to another company last week," said Walter. "The high speed dump triggered an alarm. She was a mid-level supervisor in the insurance underwriting pool on the thirty-first floor. She was altering the policy layoffs so her brother-in-law's company got all the preferred policies. What tipped us off was the first entry inserting the windows to drop out the transactions she didn't want us to see. We watched her after that and the rest was easy. We never would have caught it without the high speed system."

"So what about Jack Sullivan's money? Any ideas where it went and how they did it?"

"I know what to look for. Can't promise you anything but I have a few ideas. You see? They can destroy their own records, and they can cover their tracks by deleting computer records. However, they can't hide the telex message transferring the money to their offshore accounts, because they pay for the service, and the accountants always keep records to prove they handled it. I'll work on it piecemeal so I don't tip anyone off. Jersey Mutual never was a well-organized company, so maybe they left a few trailers around."

"Trailers?"

"Yeah, you know, stragglers, clues, fingerprints. I have ways of flushing computer systems that most programmers don't know. I'll begin the search on SARTXE. I have some ideas on where to start and I'll keep this between Kate and myself."

The girls came back around dinnertime from their tour, so we went to Arturo's: two blocks south, take a right, count three sub-basement entrances and there it is. I was still carrying the Glock on my left ankle and the Special Forces knife on my right. I knew from past experience Walter was carrying a .38 Chief's Special and Kate would have her mace and Taser just in case. I was not expecting any problems but I kept a wary eye out anyway. After all, this was New York City.

The restaurant was a favorite feeding stop for the entire area and in New York City that's saying something. Kate made reservations so when we arrived Arturo's wife, Mamie, greeted us like we were royalty and showed us to a corner booth with red and white checkered tablecloths, lighted candles in Chianti bottles, pictures on the walls of celebrities who had eaten there, and last but not least, real linen napkins.

"William, ma boy. How'a you been?" Arturo was as jolly and rotund as always.

"Not so good, Arturo," I said. "I'm feeling a little weak."

"Why? Whata you matter, my boy?" He squeezed my arms and felt my torso. It was a game we played. "You a little skinny there younga man. I gotta just the tinga for you. Set and get ready," and off he went giving orders to Mamie and his waiters. Then began the eating experience of our lives.

"I'm going to regret this, but I'm not going to worry about it tonight," Walter said.

Pascuali, our waiter, poured a light white Tuscan wine I'd not heard of, and we toasted everything in the place. It was a superb light semi-dry wine with a flavor I'd never tasted, one of those you can't quite remember afterward, but you would know it if you ever had it again because it was so distinctive. Sort of like your first love. Then came the salad bowl and individual antipastos with a variety of imported olives, prosciutto, provolone, and other cheeses you would find only in the mother country. A new item on the menu were the breaded slices of zucchini, marinated diced eggplant, deep fried ravioli and sliced pimento that actually tasted good.

"Come on, you people! Eata up! I no giva you the main course if you donna clean your plates." Arturo was adamant.

The spaghetti arrived in a big bowl, sauce with sweet sausage and meatballs on the side, fettuccine escargot, baked ravioli, lasagna, and a variety of dishes whose names I couldn't pronounce if I tried. We ate and drank and when Arturo pulled out his fiddle and Mamie sat at the piano, we danced on the sawdust-covered floor and then we ate and drank some more. It was after midnight when we left, Arturo promising to send us a bill and Walter promising to pay.

"Tomorrow I'll settle up with Mamie when everyone is sober," said Walter. "Don't worry, it's on the company and Arturo won't soak us because I send a lot of business his way."

We were strolling along, feeling no pain, enjoying the feeling of the light drizzle on our faces, when I sensed someone behind us. A man in a trench coat with his hat pulled down over his forehead, was walking about twenty paces behind. I remembered vaguely when we came up the stairs out of Arturo's that there was no one in sight in either direction, so I became suspicious. Then I saw the other one up ahead dressed the same way leaning against the building at the corner of the street.

"We got company," I said.

"I was wondering about that. What should we do?" said Walter.

"Act casual. You carrying?" I asked.

"Yeah," said Walter.

"Okay, I'm going to tie my shoe. Watch what they do but don't stare at them, understand? You girls, act silly. Giggle and laugh."

I kneeled down, and acted like I was tying my shoe while slipping the Glock out of its ankle holster. I took the two extra clips in my other hand. The trench coat behind did a sudden stop, fumbled in his pocket, and came out with a cigarette. He had obviously seen too many movies. I stood up and that's when I noticed the car, a black big four-door Lincoln Continental parked around the corner to the right where the other trench coat was standing. Exhaust was rising out of the tailpipe and the windows were open.

"There's someone in that car," I said. "Now girls, when I say dive, you jump down those stairs leading to the next sub-basement. We have to draw them in before we get too close to that car. Walter, you go with them and provide cover."

"I'll stay with you, buddy."

"No! We're better off splitting up. They'll never expect it and they're not set up for a divided field of fire. Okay, dive!"

I stepped left, blended my profile with a lamppost, steadied my weapon on the post and aimed at the guy following us. He was slow getting his gun out. I waited as long as I could as he pulled the weapon out of his pocket, and then I nailed him with two shots to the chest. He went down as I squatted and turned just in time as the other trench coat came up with an Uzi from his coat. He was fast, and as my first shot struck him he was spraying the street with bullets. I dived for the gutter, rolled and came up firing, but he was already down and crawling across the sidewalk toward the car. Then the fireworks started for real.

All four doors of the Lincoln popped open and guys with guns came pouring out shooting as they ran around the car for cover. I was still washing my face in the gutter so I didn't make a real good target but I commenced firing at everything that moved. It was a stupid gangland style street shoot out with hot lead flying everywhere. I was vaguely aware of Walter's Smith and Wesson .38 Special as he fired it from his bunker position. He did some good because I saw two of the shooters go down on his side of the car.

I rolled and fired, fired and rolled until I was on the opposite side of the street. They were lousy shots, but they had automatic weapons and you don't have to be all that great to hit something. I was on my third clip and there was one shooter left. He got the message that he was in big trouble and moved to the front of the car, firing over the hood from behind the left front headlight. I hunkered down behind a cement trashcan holder and waited for him to use up his ammo, a neat trick I'd learned the day before under fire behind the Jersey barriers at the marina. I couldn't see the other side of the car, but I thought I could out last him. "Just sit tight," I told myself as I crouched down with bullets smashing into everything around me.

Then Walter stood up and ran toward the back of the car. The shooter in front couldn't see him at first, but when Walter started to move along the left side of the car, the kid turned and almost got him. He made one big mistake when he fired at Walter, however, he stood up, and I popped him twice, steadying the Glock on the top of the trash can holder.

"You owe me another one, Walter," I muttered as I stood and walked across the street.

Suddenly, the car lurched forward, running over the kid I'd just dropped. Someone was still in the driver's seat, and before I could get a good shot at him, the car was around the next corner and gone, its two back doors still open with wounded shooters hanging out, their legs and arms dragging on the pavement as the vehicle disappeared. Walter got off two more useless shots but they were gone, leaving behind two men lying wounded on the street along with the first one I shot on the sidewalk. The NYPD was there almost before I could say, "It's stopped raining."

Now, there is one thing about the New York Police. They are a busy bunch of guys and they don't care who you are; just don't do it in their town. There are over twenty-seven thousand police in the New York metropolitan area and they all have one thing in common. They've seen every form of mischief and mayhem that humankind can produce, and they really don't care what your problem is. So we spent the rest of the night and most of the following morning under interrogation trying to convince the detectives that the bad guys were the ones that got away. It was only after Hank Gaines showed up and had a conference with the precinct chief that we got permission to leave.

"Man, this is too much, O'Keefe. I don't care if you and Walter St. Onge were knitting sweaters with a class full of nuns, you gotta stop this stuff. Man, that precinct chief wanted your tail worse than a hungry cat chasing a mouse. You can't do this kind of thing every place you go. This isn't the Middle East."

"Okay, okay, Hank. Thanks for bailing us out. Now tell me who those shooters were. Why did they go after us?" I asked.

"You don't know? The heavy hitter in the trench coat was a Chicago policeman, buddy of that fellow Sergeant Vitro Whatever

His Name was, the fellow we found dead at your cottage. He's been AWOL since the day after his buddy got killed out there. The other two were hoods from Jersey City, small time cons, all with records as long as your mama's apron strings. They're still alive but the trench coat bought it. He was a desk sergeant with a family from Chicago."

"That explains why they couldn't hit anything."

"Yeah, well, they hit a lot of things. Half the windows on the block are gone. There are only two street lights still operational and fifteen cars were terminally damaged not counting the black Lincoln. About a dozen pigeons were killed but only one alley cat was found with a hole in its head. Meanwhile, two dead bodies were discovered in the burned out black Lincoln Continental this morning over in the Jersey marshes, and there's going to be hell to pay for the storefronts that got busted on the main drag around that corner. O'Keefe, you are lethal with that little automatic whadaya call it!"

"Glock 17. It holds seventeen nine-millimeter cartridges and it's very effective. Only I have a problem, my budget for ammo this month is all used up. I need a loan."

"Up yours...Geeze, man! You gotta stop shooting people. It's getting embarrassing. People keep asking me about you. They think we're buddies."

"We are, Hank. You just don't appreciate the vast possibilities our friendship offers. Speaking of friends, have you seen Victor Cantrelli yet?"

"Not yet but I sure as hell intend to. Here's something else. Man oh man, are you gonna love this one."

"What's that, Hank?"

"That Lincoln, the one they found with the bodies. The one you and St. Onge filled with holes last night."

"Yes, what about it?"

"It's registered to Angelina Cantrelli, Senator Cantrelli's wife."

"You're right, Hank. I really love it."

CHAPTER TWENTY-TWO

WE WERE A SHABBY looking crew when we arrived back at the CIC building. Walter and Kate had a penthouse next to the offices on the fortieth floor with guest rooms for visiting dignitaries: that included us and within ten minutes Connie and I were relaxing in the sunken tub. The place could qualify as a gymnasium with its Nautilus equipment, sunken bathtub, hot spa, rub down tables, and exercise machines. The sunlight streamed through a series of skylights as breakfast was served in the glassed-in sunspace on an adjacent balcony shared with the penthouse.

"Not a bad lifestyle, huh, O'Keefe?" said Walter, pouring his coffee. "You're probably thinking how I got it made and I owe this all to you, right?" He smiled. We'd had this conversation before.

"Right, just send me a monthly check at my yacht club, or would you prefer my Swiss bank account number?"

"Whatever, but I'll tell you what my friend, last night was something else. Wow, it was just like we were back in the jungles. Man, what a high! I'm still jacked. How about you?"

"I guess I'm all right but I'm getting tired of it. Not as much fun as it used to be," I lied. Actually, it never was fun being shot at.

"You old hound dog, O'Keefe. I saw what you did. You dumped us in that cellar way entrance and then you took the heat. You drew the fire away from us. You acted as a decoy. Man, you're something else. I have to hand it to you. It was just like back there in Nam in the jungle with you leading the way. You just seemed to know where the booby traps were and you could smell the Cong, like last night, you just knew where they were."

"You're making me blush, Walter. We were a unit then. We all worked together. We were a team and I was part of it. I didn't lead anything, I just survived."

"No man, you were the unofficial leader. The guys looked to you to get them out alive and you're still doing it. You're damn good at it. Thank God you were there last night. We'd be dead, otherwise."

"If we hadn't been there last night," said Connie, "you wouldn't have been attacked. They were probably after us, Bill and me."

"Do you really think so?" asked Walter. "I'm not so sure. What do you think, Bill?" He looked at me with questioning eyes.

"It wasn't set up like an ordinary ambush where you catch the enemy in a cross fire without shooting your own people. Last night was different. They were trying to trap us, to get the drop on us front and back, and the car was placed so they could shove us into it and take off. The last thing they expected was a shoot out. The trench coat behind us didn't even have his hand on his gun. I had to wait for him to get it out. That almost cost me, because the one at the corner was faster and he was shooting his Uzi before the other one had his hand out of his pocket. The other shooters were all bottled up in the car, not spread out like a normal ambush."

"So are you saying they were trying to kidnap us?" said Kate.

"I don't know," I answered. "It seems a good possibility."

"But who were they really after?" asked Connie.

"Well, they certainly should know better than to try something that crazy with O'Keefe, especially after what he did to Anthony Pinucci's brother, Sal," said Walter.

"So they were after us?" Kate was incredulous.

"No love, they were probably after me," said Walter, his gaze settling on me, "and that's how they intend to do it, right Bill?"

"Seems likely. At first I thought it was just more of the same Neanderthal shoot 'em up stuff that Connie and I have been going through the last few days, but now that I have time to think about it, last night was different. You need to beef up security around here,

Mr. St. Onge. Looks like you've become a target again."

We finished breakfast and left the girls in the penthouse. Walter showed me some techniques for checking on Jersey Mutual's financial dealings.

"As you know, Bill, all telex messages containing highly sensitive and classified financial information are coded with a system called D.E.S. That's Data Encryption Standard, a system developed out of research done in the 1970's and approved for use by the military and National Security Agency. These codes are restricted. Only the telex rooms in major banking centers have them. Each code is based on a secret number or key and on standard formats shared by both the sending and receiving facilities. Now, it would take forever for us to go that route in order to find Jersey Mutual's transactions. We would have to break every code individually and some we might never break. But some of those transactions were done through our own telex room here at CIC and we have a file on them. I'll see where it leads me. Once we know the destination of some of their transactions, we can test out a few other theories."

We worked until lunchtime and took a break. Walter said we were making progress, although I didn't understand much of what he was doing. We agreed that he would continue to work on it, and after lunch, Connie and I headed to my cottage. It was time to go back to my roots and collect my thoughts.

"Mr. O'Keefe, I am physically and emotionally exhausted," she said, as we left Manhattan.

"I know, Babe. It feels like we've been watching one continuous fireworks display for the last six days. I need to find a place where I can launch an offensive. It makes no sense to let these attacks go unanswered."

"So, where are we going?" asked Connie.

"Back to the cottage to regroup and plan our strategy."

"I don't know, can we go some place else, like maybe the boat? I don't think I can stay at the cottage for a while after what happened there. It's not that I'm squeamish. It's just...well...I think we should give it some time before we go back there."

"Okay, then, it's the boat. Maybe we can even get some serious sailing in now that the rain has stopped."

"I would like that. I really would," and I knew what she meant.

Connie leaned over against the right window and fell asleep. There were a lot of cars on the LIE but everything was moving. I had time to think as I drove and what I had to consider was not too encouraging. SARTXE was a very illusive and powerful organization, but not really an organization. It was more like a conspiracy, its activities buried deeply within our financial, business, and political institutions. If it came to a showdown who would they believe, an ambassador to the United Nations, a president of the World Bank, an advisor to the President of the United States of America, an admiral in the Pentagon?

Against all these was a beat up, worn out, divorced, trigger-happy insurance investigator with a reputation for cutting corners, doing things a bit on the shady side of the law and no permanent residence or telephone listing. No, my position was definitely not a strong one. If something didn't break my way soon, the children would be orphans, Jack and Judith Sullivan would be on welfare, Connie would be a free woman, the Nature Conservancy Watch Committee would have my cottage torn down, and my boat would be in probate with no one to take care of it. There just was no justice in this world!

All was quiet at the marina and Tom Green assured me no one had been near my boat as he handed over my messages. Perkins General Store was undergoing reconstruction and someone had thoughtfully cleaned up the street, which included removing the white tape outlining the position of the bodies. I opened the boat to air it out and we settled into an unusually quiet evening. I puttered around, scrubbing the decks and cleaning the hardware while Connie continued her nap...post battle-shock syndrome. I'd seen it before. I finally stretched out in the cockpit with a triple shot of Ole Hound Dog Kentucky Straight Bourbon and fell asleep...my solution to post battle shock syndrome.

It was dark when I woke up and I found Connie sitting on the other side of the cockpit looking at me.

"Hi, sorry if I woke you," she said.

"No problem. I must have dozed off. Didn't mean to."

She hesitated, and then said, "Bill, we have to talk. I simply cannot go on like this any longer. I thought I could but it's just too brutal. I'm not accustomed to seeing dead bodies every other day and being shot at between lunch and dinner, breakfast and lunch or whatever. It's thrown me all off schedule and then there's the problem of having to sleep in a different bed every night and not sleeping at all some nights.

I don't know how you do it, William Thackery O'Keefe. You are incredible. I mean...well...it's like you actually thrive on this sort of insanity. It seems to charge your batteries so that you go forever, catching a little sleep here or there, eating now and then, taking a shower on impulse wherever the opportunity arises. You never seem to run out of ammunition and nothing ever slows you down. You're some piece of work and I love you, but I just cannot keep it up. I need a breather."

"Do you want to take off for awhile? Maybe go home?"

"I can't go back to my place no matter what condition it's in."

"Yes I know that. I mean home, as in Wilson, Iowa, where your family lives. You know what I mean, Connie Wilson of Wilson, Iowa? Maybe you need to go home, to your roots, to where you were born and raised. Get three good squares a day, sleep at night, and church on Sunday, just until you get your feet on the ground and get centered again."

"I don't know about that. I don't think I could leave you right in the middle of all this with no one to talk to, no one to stand by your side."

"Sometimes I work better alone, Connie."

"Well, I don't and I couldn't possibly leave you this way. I think maybe I should stay. You'll need me. You'll see." She yawned. "I'll need you too. It's better this way. I just have to get a good night's sleep and maybe a little loving. That'll do it. You'll see." She stood and went to the main hatch. Halfway down the ladder she stopped and said, "I'm glad we had this little talk, aren't you?"

I said yes and watched her as she crawled back into the portside bunk and fell asleep. I decided to check my messages and make some calls. The note on top was from Jack Chusak. I called him back from the pay phone and got an earful.

"O'Keefe, where have you been? I've been calling all over trying to find you. Then I hear you're in New York City last night and you shot the man who is the reason I was trying to get hold of you. Man, you are something else."

"What are you talking about?" I said.

"Look, I've been working overtime trying to nail this SARTXE thing. I traced those names you gave me and nearly got my head chopped off. I requested a file on Admiral Rassmussen and got a visit from the FBI instead. I tried a credit check on Ambassador Malcome Kitterage and got another visit from the FBI. Then I checked that telephone number in Champaign and found out it was a drop line with call forwarding to an office of State Mutual Insurance in Omaha, Nebraska. On the way back to my office from Champaign, some turkey tried to kill me with a shotgun. Drove right up along side of me on the Outer Belt Highway and blew my back window out. It would have been my head if I hadn't seen him. So I chased the jerk and ran him off the road and now he's a corpse and I'm ticked. What the hell's goin' on here anyway?" He was yelling.

"You tripped some alarm wires. These people are very touchy. You mentioned something about the reason you were trying to call me."

"Yeah, I ran across a clue regarding the guy you found dead at your cottage, Sergeant Vitro Alexander. He was reported AWOL along with two of his colleagues. They were identified as being on a flight to Providence on July Fourth. I have their names. Then I get a call this morning from this Chief of Police, Baumgarten, in Chicago. Seems you shot one of them last night in New York City. His name is Ira Sommers and he's a pal of this Sergeant Alexander. The third man, whom I am told you probably wounded and then let get away, is Ira's brother-in-law, a Lieutenant Joseph Sontaigm, who is also AWOL from the Chicago Police Department. Boy, you sure know how to pick em."

"You don't realize it, Jack, but you just tied up a loose end that's been bothering me. Does the name Samuel Sontaigm mean anything to you?"

"Sure, he's an advisor to the President and...hey, you're right! He's from Champaign, Illinois. He's real big down there. So you're saying he's probably related to this Lieutenant Joseph Sontaigm? No wonder someone is shooting at me."

"It works for me, Jack. It explains why so much of this mess leads to Chicago and the drop line to Omaha implicates my old boss, John Stanley, who was a protégé of Samuel Sontaigm in the old days. Now, what about John Delmar?"

"I'm working on that, and when I get it nailed down, I'm gonna flush him down the drain with whoever is in on it with him."

"That sounds right to me."

I now had the broad outlines of the puzzle with some pieces in their proper places. If Lieutenant Joseph Sontaigm of the Chicago P.D. was related to the Samuel Sontaigm of Presidential advisor fame, then I had the strongest connection there was to tie SARTXE into the plan that Jack Sullivan was supposed to be working on as well as the attempts on my life. The fact that Sontaigm's brother was in on the shooting in New York City where the getaway car was registered to Angelina Cantrelli, the senator's wife, provided a very strong linkage between Sontaigm and Cantrelli. Problem was I might never be able to touch these people.

Ambassador Kitterage and Admiral Rassmussen had flags on their files to keep anyone away from investigating them. Jack Chusak found that out the hard way. Then there was the telephone number in Champaign, Illinois, a drop line with call forwarding to an office inside the State Mutual Insurance headquarters in Omaha. My old boss John Stanley, president and CEO of State Mutual was the heavy there. He said they would get me and they certainly had tried. Sontaigm had been his stockbroker. He would probably slither out from under any investigation of SARTXE when the rock was lifted. John was good at slithering away when things got hot.

The next message said my kids had called. I dialed the number of the estate and reversed charges. Natalie answered and I got an earful of pain and suffering. The woman just didn't know how to live without complaining. Eventually, she ran out of breath and Samantha came on the line. We talked for about ten minutes and she said she loved me. Jonathan said he was bored and wanted to come see me. Timothy said the same but I could feel the hurt and the loneliness in his voice.

"Son," I said, "whenever you need me, I'll be there."

Little did I know, those were the most important words I would ever utter in my entire life.

CHAPTER TWENTY-THREE

IT WAS LATE WHEN I returned to the boat. Arnold Perkins wanted to tell me his son, Gerry, was doing well and would be home from the hospital soon. Tom Green had a few questions about some custom made swivel blocks I'd ordered. Did I want rosewood or teak? I told him I wanted strong wood and to ask for locust. Harry Gomes wanted to relate that his sister, Ginger, had asked for me and I said "hello" back, experiencing a pleasant moment as I recalled our voyage together last year. Ginger was a man's dream. I had a drink with Marty and Grace Gomes and then went to my bunk. Connie was still out of it, 'just getting a good night's sleep'. Somewhere in the night I fell asleep, and the next few hours of fitful slumber became the last I would have for quite awhile.

Tom Green woke me just before daylight with a cryptic, "Phone call!" I went to the office and said hello.

"O'Keefe? Kim Woo here. Your children have been kidnapped!"

The intruders had landed on the airstrip in an Otter: engine out, six of them, about an hour before dawn. Agent Joe Thomas was dead. Agent Corsini was wounded but walking. Natalie was hysterical. Woo could have a plane down to pick me up in forty-five minutes. I told him I'd be at Orient Point and said goodbye. Connie was dressed and had hot coffee on when I returned to the boat. My clothes were laid out on the bunk. The Glock and the .44 Magnum were next to them with extra ammo.

"Tom told me what's going on. Ready when you are," she said.

The Charles Rose airport at Orient Point is small and private. The north end of the short grass runway ends at the water. I recognized Jack Sullivan's new twin Beech as it turned on final for landing. Woo opened the door and waved us in with the engines running and we were taxiing to the end of the small grass strip for takeoff before we even had our seat belts fastened.

"This is Kenny Warren...Bill and Connie." Woo made the introductions. The pilot looked familiar. "You may remember him," said Woo. "Those were his helicopters that were blown up on the runway at the Sullivan's on July Fourth."

Then I remembered. It was his pilot and helicopter.

"Sorry about your pilot," I said, not knowing what else to say.

"My brother," said Kenny as he checked the mags, lowered the flaps to forty percent, centered on the runway, and prepared for a short field takeoff. "He was a good pilot," Kenny said as he applied full power and released the brakes.

We bounced down the runway...heavy...the wheels seeming reluctant to leave the ground. Then when all seemed lost and the end of the runway and the water were coming at us like the end of the world, we were airborne, gear coming up, Kenny adjusting power, syncing the props, bleeding flaps, and suddenly we were in a smooth left turn climbing out over the water. We were in the hands of a pro, and as Kenny leveled out at thirty-five hundred feet and pointed it northwest, I had a sense that we were rushing into the jaws of hell.

"I was going to Albany when I heard the call," said Kim. "I cancelled my class at the university and headed up to the Sullivan estate. The place was in a shambles. Joe Thomas was dead in the upstairs hallway, Corsini was semi-conscious in the guest bedroom, and your ex-wife was out of control. They cut the wires on the phone but the maid kept her head. She stopped the bleeding in Corsini's shoulder and sent the gardener down the road to call it in. I got there before the locals and did what I could. I called Kenny because he lives just over the hill. Then I called you. Lucky I had a phone."

"It was one of those big radials," said Kenny. I heard them take off, so I jumped outta bed and saw it goin' north toward Bear Mountain.

It was a DeHavilan Otter. Not many of them around here. They went straight up the river toward Albany."

We left Long Island Sound behind, passed southeast of White Plains, went over the Croton Reservoir and let down onto the airstrip behind the estate. Our landing was on the numbers at the approach end of the runway.

"Nice landing," I said.

"Nice runway," said Kenny.

"Nice airplane," said Connie.

"Nice day," said Woo.

"Not for long," I responded.

The estate was crawling with police and medics. The medical examiner was just finishing and he was in no mood to chat. I got the basics and the rest came from Corsini. He was asleep when they came into the house and up the stairs. It was the same bunch that did the robbery on July 4th. Corsini didn't have his gun next to the bed so he had to get up and find it. He was stumbling around in the closet on his hands and knees when they came through the bedroom door firing at the bed and everything else in the room. He passed out when he realized he was hit. Joe Thomas was in the hallway outside Natalie's bedroom, naked and dead, a Colt Detective Special in his right hand, all six chambers fired. His body had thirty-seven bullet holes that could be counted. The medical examiner thought one or more of the intruders had been wounded by Thomas' gunfire.

The children were taken in their pajamas. I checked their rooms and found signs of a struggle in Timothy's bed, but no blood. Natalie was inconsolable. When she saw me she became hysterical, screaming that it was my fault. I listened for a few moments then I lost my cool.

"You selfish witch!" I yelled. "Joe Thomas was an FBI agent on duty. It was his job to protect you and the children. It was not his job to sleep with you. It wasn't enough for you to subjugate the children to your vicious, sick control was it? You had to prove you could do it to Joe Thomas. Well congratulations, lady. Because of you they're gone. If I'd been here, this never would have happened. That stairwell would be littered with dead terrorists."

I said a few other things, which were meant to hurt and I think she actually heard some of it. I couldn't believe she'd taken advantage of the situation by distracting Agent Thomas from his job. He was weak, as any man would have been in the presence of a woman with Natalie's attributes. If you could get past her totally selfish and abrasive personality, there was a woman endowed with a body far beyond a man's wildest dreams, and if she chose to lower herself, she could satisfy the hungriest man alive. It was her vicious, self-centered, unpredictable behavior that turned people off. Evidently, she hid that part of herself from Joe or maybe he just didn't care. Now it was too late, and the ball was in my court. I had to separate my personal feelings from my professional judgments now and take control.

"Corsini wants to see you," said Kim. "He's in Mr. Sullivan's office."

We went downstairs and found Corsini sitting in Jack's chair talking on the phone, a bandage on his left shoulder. Evidently, phone service had been restored. He didn't fill Jack's chair as far as I was concerned and I resented him sitting there. We waited for him to hang up.

"O'Keefe, I'm really sorry about this mess. It never should have happened, but we've got to move on, right? I just finished talking to the Director. A team is on its way even as we speak. We'll have this thing nailed down in no time. Look...ahh...why don't you have a seat, okay? This may take some time. It was those terrorists again, just like before. This makes it a terrorist kidnapping." It seemed important for him to classify it. "Good, now, there's a message...ahh...evidently for you, O'Keefe. It was tacked on the front door. Weird, but that's where they left it. I can't let you see it, of course, until forensics has a look..."

"What does it say?"

"Well, I can't reveal that until..."

"What's the damned message say, you jerk?" I grabbed Corsini by the throat and lifted him out of the chair.

"I...arrgh..."

"Speak to me you stupid wimp. You stood around and let your partner prong my ex-wife when he should have been protecting those children. Did she do you too?" The look on his face told it all. "You pitiful piece of shit!" I said.

Woo put his hand lightly on my shoulder and squeezed. I let Corsini go reluctantly, dropping him hard into the chair. The message was on the desk inside a clear plastic folder. I picked it up and read it.

"Give it up or you won't see your children again," it said.

It was done on a cheap laser printer. Not easily traced, and for that matter the message was meaningless. It would take an idiot to miss the meaning of this kidnapping. I dropped it back on the desk and looked at Corsini. He was useless. He'd regressed back into his bureaucratic mode. He was not a field operative, he was an administrative type, a reader, and worse yet, a party-liner.

"Terrorists, shit, Corsini! You're lucky they weren't real terrorists. You would be liver pate´ right now instead of sitting in that chair, all puffed up with importance over talking to the Director. Hell, you wouldn't know a lousy terrorist if he walked up and handed you a custom made bomb."

His wound was bleeding, his face was pale, and I could see that he didn't feel well, but I cared less. I was about to tell him to go lay down and do what he obviously did best, which was screw off, when his body suddenly tilted forward and he passed out, his head hitting the desk with a thwacking sound. Woo gave me a hand and we carried him upstairs to the spare bedroom, tossed him on the bed, and shut the door. The M.E. wanted to know if we had another body but I told him Corsini wasn't dead...yet!

"Do you think he will bleed to death?" asked Woo.

"I hope so," I said. "Geeze! Can you figure that, an FBI agent who leaves his gun in the closet and goes to bed, hears gun fire, stumbles around in the dark trying to find his gun. He survives because he's on his knees groping for it inside the closet when the intruders smash open the door and chop up everything in the room with AK-47s. The little jerk will probably get an award for outsmarting his attackers. His behavior will be studied at the FBI academy as a new way of surviving a terrorist attack. Can you imagine the reaction to the directive instructing all FBI agents to leave their guns in the closet from now on?"

"You're just sour grapes because they didn't give you an award for shooting down that chopper full of so-called terrorists," said Woo.

"I don't need awards to know that I did it right. If I'm still alive and I have all my body parts after an engagement, my friend, that's doing it right," I replied.

"Didn't you receive awards for what you did in Viet Nam?"

"What my unit did in Nam was unofficial, so we received no recognition for it, no pats on the back. That was part of the deal when we volunteered and it was all right with us because we were a team and we were our own reward. When we did it right, we knew it and when we didn't, we took corrective action."

"Sounds like you were proud of what you did," said Woo.

"Not really but we were proud of our unit. What we did mostly doesn't bear repeating, but who we were was a proud fighting unit." I looked at Kim Woo and caught a glint of understanding in his eyes and something prompted me to ask, "Have you ever been under fire?"

He hesitated then said simply, "Yes."

"Where?"

"Nicaragua...El Salvador...Angola...Afghanistan, a few other places." His expression was blank.

"I thought you were just an Air Force intelligence type."

"I was, but it got boring so I volunteered. I wanted more excitement."

"Sounds like you got it."

"Yeah, you might say that," he said, looking away.

We went for a walk and talked. Connie was with Natalie trying to calm her down. I shared my revelations on SARTXE with Woo and the connections involving Cantrelli, Pinucci, Sontaigm, Stanley, Rassmussen, and Kitterage as well as the shooters, the Chicago-Omaha connection and the Navy Seals. Woo absorbed it all, nodding his head when he understood, asking short, penetrating questions when he didn't. I saw that he could be a very sharp interrogator.

"Sounds like they cleaned out Jack Sullivan's financial holdings and then the President chose him to head up the plan to milk the drug cartels. Then Jack brought you into it and they panicked. After that East Harbour episode, which cost them millions, you were the last person they wanted around."

"I never pictured myself as being all that important. I mean, they could have waited and I would have been gone. Then they could have done what they wanted," I said.

"Maybe," said Woo, "but they didn't know that. You pose a threat to them in several ways. They probably had no idea you were related to Jack Sullivan when they filched his money. It's amazing how poorly informed crooks can be when they pull a scam. Then, there's your habit of decimating their ranks whenever you meet up with them. I can't imagine that they can afford to lose any more of their operatives."

"Why do you say that? They seem to have plenty of shooters."

"Not really," said Woo, his analytical skills kicking in. "Those guys they sent against you were really heavy types. Think about it. There were two sergeants from the Chicago Police Department and one detective lieutenant who turns out, we suppose, to be the brother of a presidential advisor. Then there is the brother of the president and CEO of one of the largest and best-known insurance companies in this area, and a personal bodyguard to a well-known and influential United States senator. These are not cheap hoods. They're family, insiders who have a direct blood tie to the principals in SARTXE. They wouldn't be wasting their last and best troops if they had other resources. The attack on Connie's apartment by what appears to be Navy Seals is interesting. I'm wondering if there are some blood ties there also," said Woo.

"You mean some relative of Admiral Rassmussen or Senator Cantrelli might be a Navy Seal? That should be easy enough to check."

"Yeah, I still have contacts in the Pentagon," said Woo, "and believe me, this time the FBI will not come visiting when I make inquiries about these people."

We walked for a while longer, speculating about the kidnapping and where they might be holding the children. We came to no conclusions by the time we returned to the main house and I was feeling frustrated. Connie came frantically running from the office when we opened the door and stepped into the main hall,

"Bill, oh thank God. Come quick. It's Kate on the telephone. They've kidnapped Walter St. Onge."

CHAPTER TWENTY-FOUR

KIM WOO HANDLED HIS car like a professional racecar driver. We made it to the CIC building in record time just before noon. The penthouse was a mess and Kate was in bad shape although she had no physical injuries

"They came in by helicopter and down the side of the building on ropes, smashed through the triple glazed sunspace glass and went directly for the bedroom." Stan Paulsen, head of security, was a short, stocky man in his fifties. He continued, "They fired at the glass and at the bedroom door because it was locked and that was it, minimal shooting. Mr. St. Onge realized he was under attack and pushed Kate out of bed, fired his handgun several times at his attackers, and was knocked unconscious. He hit one of them, wounded him pretty bad, as you can see." He pointed at a trail of blood on the rug. "They left a note, says, 'Don't call the police, we'll be in touch'." He handed it to me. It was printed by a cheap laser printer on computer paper.

"These people have brass," I said handing the note back to Stan.

"I see what you mean, a Stoner-50. These guys are real pros. It pays to send the very best." Kim said holding several shell casings in his hand.

"They're ahead of us, that's for sure," said Stan. "Who ever heard of industrial espionage using terrorist methods like this? What the hell am I supposed to do with this mess?"

"For starters I suggest you call the police and get the FBI involved," I said. "In spite of what that note says, you're not going to crack this case alone. Besides, it's connected to the kidnapping of my children this morning up in Westchester County and the FBI is already in on that case."

"But they said not to call the police," he said.

"Right, Stan, and if something happens to Walter St. Onge, what are you going to tell the police, that you decided all on your own to keep it a secret? You could get hung out to dry forever."

"I understand all that, but Kate might have something to say about it. She says not to call the police because the kidnappers will kill him."

"She'll change her mind when she hears what they're doing."

I went to the living room where Connie was consoling Kate. I noticed Kim Woo on the telephone as I came into the room.

"Bill, I think I should stay here with Kate for awhile. I don't think she wants to be alone," said Connie.

"Sure, Babe, I think that would be a good thing. I may have something to do on my own anyway. Meanwhile, Kate, I think you should call in the police. Stan Paulsen can discuss it with you but I'm sure Walter would agree. We need their help. Connie can fill you in on what's happened."

"Oh, God! No! They'll kill him. I'll never see Walter again. You don't understand." Kate was not herself.

"Kate, listen to me! These people are very powerful and well organized and we can't fight them alone. Another thing you might consider is this. If we don't document this kidnapping they'll get away with it, and no one will be the wiser. One thing for sure, the FBI is good at documenting evidence. Anyway, I have some things to do and I'd feel better if you had police protection while I'm gone."

"For some reason, this doesn't sound too good. Are you planning a mission or something, or should I not ask?" said Connie.

"Don't ask. You really don't want to know," I said.

Woo hung up the phone. "We have another link. You'll never guess what I just turned up. A buddy at the Pentagon did some quick checks for me. Seems Admiral Rassmussen was a Navy Seal in Viet Nam. He went up the ladder pretty fast after the war, and one of his students was Victor Cantrelli in the early 1960's before Viet Nam heated up. Now get this. Admiral Rassmussen has a very unusual specialty in the Navy. He is in charge of procurement, which doesn't sound very glamorous, but one of his responsibilities is to test and evaluate various products and systems and report back on them. He can requisition almost anything he wants. He recently borrowed five Stoner-50s with ammo for some project."

"How the hell did he get away with that?" I said.

"He has a lot of pull, and it seems there was a top secret memo from the White House directing the temporary transfer of any men or materials necessary for the Admiral's use, and guess who one of the men was who was transferred? It just happens to be one Victor Cantrelli, Jr., who is presently a Navy Seal team leader. He's on detached duty to Admiral Rassmussen." Woo raised his eyebrows for emphasis.

"What, doesn't anyone question this sort of stuff?" asked Connie. "Senator Cantrelli has a son who is a Navy Seal team leader and they send him and five of these rock things someplace and no one questions it?"

"Those are Stoners," I said. "They're automatic weapons with an unbelievable capacity for destruction. Damn! So Sontaigm just happens to arrange for the transfer of this junior Cantrelli to Admiral Rassmussen, who is part of SARTXE, and we have two attacks in the last week by someone using Seal team weapons and tactics. Ladies and gentlemen, I think the FBI will be very interested in this one."

I went to the telephone and dialed a private number from memory, to which very few people had access. It rang once.

"Yes?" Hank Gaines answered.

"O'Keefe here, got a minute?" I told him everything.

"I'll alert the FBI on the CIC break-in and kidnapping," said Hank. "I think they should go after these people. Besides, they would have better access to the President in order to determine just how much he actually knows about SARTXE and its principals. He might be in on it, you know?"

"I don't want to believe that," I said. "I know it needs to be verified and the FBI can do it. By the way, what about Senator Cantrelli? Did you and the state attorney have your talk with him?"

"Would you believe Senator Victor Cantrelli is among the missing? We went to his Brooklyn office to interview him like we arranged and the son of a lizard wasn't there. His secretary informed us he was on a Caribbean vacation and couldn't be reached. Just to make sure, we checked his Georgetown Condo and his Rensselaer home. He hasn't been seen anywhere since the July 4th picnic at the Sullivan's Westchester estate, and that includes the hospital where he and his dying bodyguard never showed up. He's gone to ground now and he left no trail."

I took Woo aside and said, "I'm going hunting. I may bend a few laws and violate a few people's human rights. I don't know how squeamish you might be, but you're welcome to come along. Just don't get in the way. I have my own methods of investigating."

"No problem, O'Keefe. I have the day off, so I'll pretend I'm not a law enforcement officer. Lead the way," he said.

I left Kate and Connie with Stan Paulsen. We crossed the East River on the Manhattan Bridge, went down Flatbush Avenue, and started looking for the address I wanted. It was in the Bensonhurst area. I'd been in Brooklyn many times but I always went to a definite place, like the Brooklyn Hospital, the Botanic Gardens or the aquarium out on Coney Island. I wasn't familiar with the residential areas but Woo seemed right at home.

"We're in the heart of old Brooklyn. This area has been reclaimed," said Woo. "Cantrelli's headquarters is right there, across the street. Looks quiet from here but it may be heavily guarded."

I glanced at the notebook in my hand. "Over there is the address of Anthony Torleni, the man I shot at Green's Marina. Looks like he lived right next door to Cantrelli. Salvatore Pinucci, the other shooter, lived across the street. There's a whole nest of them all living next to each other on the same block."

We left the car and walked across the street. Large maple trees grew through holes in the cement sidewalk. The trees had grown too big for the original size of the holes and the slabs of the sidewalk were heaved up by the roots of each tree. Much work had been done on the old brownstones so they actually looked spiffy. I tried the front door of Cantrelli's house, but it was locked, so I punched the bell button several times. After the third ring, the etched glass door opened and revealed the diminutive form of an old man in a black tux with tails.

"A butler, by God," Woo exclaimed in a whisper.

"May I help you, gentlemen?" He appraised us head to toe.

"We're from Chicago. I think we're expected," I tried to un-educate my words, tough guy-like.

"You don't look like the Chicago group. What sort of uniform is that one wearing?"

"It's a disguise for the next operation. Come on Pops, don't leave us out here in the damned street." It worked and he stepped aside.

"Where's the boss? We gotta talk to him. Got a message for him."

"I suppose you are referring to the Senator, sir. I am sorry but he is not available."

"Not available or not here? Which one is it?"

"Both, I'm afraid sir. Will you be staying? You have no luggage."

"It's outside. We thought we'd check the accommodations here first. They said you'd have rooms for us."

The interior of the house was old and rich. The woodwork was the original natural beech-wood and oak of the mid-Victorian style, when houses were built the right way. The original ornate cast iron radiators were painted gold and the walls were covered in complex paisley red velvet. We followed the old man around the central carpeted stairway to an elevator in the hallway, which led to the back of the house. The elevator opened on the top or fourth floor and we stepped out. The decor there was more Spartan. The original old swivel gas light fixtures decorated the plain horsehair plaster walls of the main hallway and there was a musty smell to it all.

"You can stay in this room, gentlemen. I'll bring your luggage up whenever you wish. If there is anything you need, I'll be downstairs. There is an intercom on the wall. I'm sure you can figure out how to work it," he said with slight sarcasm in his voice.

"When do we eat?" asked Kim.

"Martha will bring your dinner at six o'clock. I'll let you know when your orders arrive." He turned and stepped into the elevator.

"What the hell are we doing here, O'Keefe? If they find out who we are, they'll pull our fingernails out and hang us by our ears," Kim said, punching the elevator button, but it didn't work. We were locked

in. “Are you sure you have a plan?”
I just shrugged and looked around.
“I’m working on it,” I replied.

CHAPTER TWENTY-FIVE

KIM HAD A GOOD point. We'd bluffed our way into the lion's den and now we had to think about what to do next. As a deputy sheriff, Kim was sworn to uphold the law of the land and that was a problem right now. He needed an attitude adjustment.

"Come on, let's check this place out," I said. Keep your gun handy, we may have to blast our way out of here."

"Get serious, O'Keefe. We're trapped. They locked out the elevator and there are no fire escapes."

"Stop your complaining. What would you do if this was a foreign country and you were on a mission?"

"That doesn't work here. We're in the United States of America and I'm a deputy sheriff." I let it go and went to work.

We checked all the rooms on the top floor and found them empty. A narrow stairway led down the back to the next floor with a locked door at the bottom. I managed to open the old lock, but something else was holding the door shut from the other side, a deadbolt or maybe it was nailed shut. We backtracked and went to the elevator.

"What do we do now, Mr. Smartass?" asked Woo. "We've walked right into a trap and we're prisoners up here."

"You gotta think positive, deputy. Obviously, you have no experience at breaking and entering."

"No kidding," he said.

I took a small tool kit out of my pocket and unscrewed the key plate on the wall next to the elevator door jam. It was a standard three-wire system and I simply shorted the wires. The elevator motor activated and the light behind the up arrow glowed brightly. After a few seconds the elevator door opened and we stepped in. I pressed the third floor button and down we went. When the door opened, I flipped the power switch to off and the door stayed open as we stepped off onto the plush red carpet. The third floor was newly renovated. The woodwork smelled of fresh paint and the ceiling was white. The walls sported modern vertically striped wallpaper. Modern fixtures lighted the hallway and there were light switches instead of gas fixtures like on the floor upstairs.

I motioned Woo to the left and I took the right. The first three rooms were used for offices and storage space. The fourth room was pay dirt. A man with a pale face lay on an old hospital bed, a bloody bandage across his chest where my bullet had struck him. Lieutenant Joseph Sontaigm of the Chicago PD was definitely in bad shape. He looked at me with glazed eyes.

"Who are you?" he asked.

"I'm your replacement."

"Good luck," he said. "That O'Keefe is one dangerous SOB."

"So tell me about him. What went wrong?" I said.

"We had bad intelligence. We didn't know who we were dealing with. We had the trap all set. We would have gotten St. Onge and his bride, no problem, but he was with that O'Keefe. I never saw anybody move so fast. It was like he smelled the trap. He's too good. If you get a chance, don't wait, take him out. Don't give him a chance or he'll nail you. He's already wiped out most of the squad. We don't have anyone left." He stopped talking as a wracking cough struck him. Kim came into the room while I waited for him to stop.

"Is this one of the boys you were looking for?" asked Kim.

"Yes." I answered as the coughing stopped.

"Who's that?" asked Sontaigm. "Is he a cop?"

"My partner. That's a disguise we're going to use to get O'Keefe. We just wanted to double-check some details with you. For instance, what kind of weapon did he use to come at you? How did he handle himself? What sort of target did he present?"

"Semi-automatic hand gun, probably nine millimeter or .38 special: lots of capacity, one of those new ones. He fired and ran, fired and rolled, fired on the run, hid behind a trashcan and a lamppost. He was tough. I've never seen anyone so accurate while he was moving. Ira never even got off a shot. That bastard shot him before he got his gun out of his pocket."

"You mean to tell me you and Ira didn't have your weapons ready?" I asked.

" Yeah, well.... We had to act natural...didn't want to tip 'em off..."

"So someone else has to go up against him and he's on guard now that you guys missed."

"It's not our fault. We didn't know O'Keefe was there. Even the two guineas missed him out on Long Island and they were using M-16s."

"Where were you going to take St. Onge and his wife when you got them?"

"Here at first and then up to the hunting camp," he said.

"The hunting camp?" I said.

"Yeah, the one up state where the Senator lives. Didn't they tell ya? The hunting camp up near Albany, the one where they were gonna take the kids and the mercs. Hey, you sure you guys know what's goin' on? How come you don't know all this stuff?"

"Man, we were called off a job in San Francisco to come here and put out this fire. We haven't been briefed on anything. We just got here, and they said to talk to you because you're the only one who's seen this O'Keefe in action and lived to tell about it. I don't like this. It's a lousy mess. We are gonna cost them extra to get this one straightened out, right Kim?"

"You bet, boss," said Kim, laying it on a bit thick.

"You know where this so-called hunting camp is located?" I asked.

"No, I was supposed to go there but I can't travel right now. The doc told me I'd have to wait about a week before I can go home. I'm all done here."

"What's your standing back in Chicago? You still have a job?"

"Hell yes! They fixed it with the Chief. He's one of us now. He's about to retire and he doesn't need any problems," he said.

"So what are they planning to do with St. Onge and those kids?" I asked, trying to control my rage.

"Set a trap for O'Keefe. You should know that. Then after you ace O'Keefe, they off the kids and St. Onge. They're useless after that, right? Then they institute the plan. Man can you believe it? We'll be zillionaires. We'll own the world." He started coughing again.

"Where's the plan now? You know, the papers they got up in Westchester on the Fourth of July?"

"Cantrelli's got them. He's supposed to give them back to my brother Sam at the next meeting. Man, who are you anyway?" Didn't they tell you anything?"

"Joseph," I said quietly. "Do you realize how many troops have been lost? Where the hell is everybody? You are the only one here. This O'Keefe is a one-man killing machine and all the big boys have run for cover. We're it, buster. We're the only ones left and if we don't do the job right this time, it could be all over. There won't be any zillion dollars for anybody. Think about it. Without us, the big boys will fall flat on their faces."

"Yeah, that's for sure. We make it happen, right?"

"Right," and I left before I gave in to the impulse to strangle the jerk.

Kim was right behind me and I had the distinct feeling that time was running out. I was in a cold rage. I wanted revenge and now there was nothing that would stand in the way of my finding Walter St. Onge and my children. These bad guys made a very big mistake when they started kidnapping people near and dear to my heart. Enough is enough!

"What's in the other rooms?" I asked Kim.

"Just paint cans and drop cloths, ladders and saw horses. They're redecorating."

I opened a couple of the doors before I found what I wanted: a five gallon can of paint thinner and two plastic jugs full of alcohol. I took them, headed for the elevator and punched the first floor button.

"Go get the car. I'll meet you outside," I said to Kim.

"You sure about this? Maybe they could search this place and pick up some clues or something." Woo just didn't get it but he would.

"I'll give you a clue, Kim. If they find out we've been here and gone, they'll move those kids and we'll never find them. It'll take them hours to sort this out when I get through. Now get outta here!"

The door was hardly open and Woo was moving. I shut the elevator off and began pouring the alcohol and paint thinner all around the first floor. I didn't really want to trap any of the servants inside, but I figured they probably had a back entrance so I lit the match and watched the fire catch and spread. Then I propped the front door open to provide a good draft and left. It was a shame to burn the old brownstone but my granddad always said, "When you find a nest of rats, the only way to make sure you get 'em all is to soak 'em in kerosene and set 'em on fire." If you've ever had rats in your cellar, you'll know what he meant.

"I hope my boss never hears about this. He'll hang me by my private parts," said Woo.

"I told you this was going to be different. When you were working for the CIA in all those exotic places: Afghanistan, Angola, Nicaragua, did you ever question what you were doing?"

"Sometimes, but I thought it was different. Those were wars. I had a mission to perform and I was military. In this country, I'm sworn to uphold the law no matter what happens."

"Wrong, Kim, this is the war. We're dealing with paramilitary hit squads, Navy Seals, guys with M-16s, AK-47s, and Uzi's. If you can't recognize a war when you see one, then you're not as good an intelligence agent as I think maybe you are."

"You're right, I know a war when I see it and that's why I'm here instead of in Albany teaching a criminology class. I guess I'm getting tired of this bureaucratic baloney. I spend ninety percent of my time training, reading, doing paper work, filing paper work, shredding paperwork, and dodging paper work. I'm not sure I do anything useful in the span of a week or a month, and when I cash my paycheck, I feel like a thief."

"More likely you feel useless, unfulfilled, and lost. You're young and you've been to the very edge. You're a warrior without a war, a Sir Galahad without a Holy Grail, a Lancelot without a damsel in distress, a rebel without a cause. You're not a thief, you're just out of time and out of place."

We made our way up the Bronx River Parkway and connected with Rt. 9 at Ossining. Traffic was picking up and time was running out. We had several options. Woo wanted to tell the FBI about the location of the kidnappers. I pointed out to him that it wouldn't work.

"They'll take an army of agents and marshals, surround the place while some bureaucrat with a bull horn stands up and broadcasts, 'This is the FBI. Come out with your hands up!' Now, I ask you, what would you do if you were a team of Navy Seals with Stoner-50s, a helicopter, a team of Cuban mercenaries with AK-47s, and all the firepower and explosives you needed? Would you come out with your hands up and face life in prison? What we need here is a classic cutting-out operation..."

"And let me guess," said Woo, "you're just the guy to do it, right?"

"We, pal, we are the ones to do the job but we need some firepower and transport. You and me, we can do it ourselves, get those kids and Walter out of that hunting camp and then let the FBI chase whatever is left."

"Geeze, O'Keefe, you never give up, do you?"

"You wanted excitement, right? So follow me."

"Yeah, okay, but maybe I should call my lawyer first and make a will," he said, shaking his head.

We stopped at a gun shop and picked up some extra ammo and a few items we thought we might need, like a flare gun with spare flares, a pair of wire cutters, one hundred feet of clothesline, night binoculars and two flashlights; basic tools like pliers, a screwdriver, an adjustable wrench, and a box of Snickers candy bars. Woo called Kenny Warren, told him what we had in mind, and he promised to meet us at the estate.

"I have a friend in Schenectady who will meet us with a car and some extra firepower. I just called him and he says it's cool," Woo said. "He knows about Cantrelli's hunting lodge and where it is. He says it's surrounded with a six foot high cattle fence but he doesn't think it's wired."

"This friend of yours, does he understand what he's getting into? Can you trust him under fire?"

"I explained it all to him. He's okay and I'll vouch for him. He's my brother," said Kim, as he stepped on the gas.

CHAPTER TWENTY-SIX

THE SULLIVAN ESTATE WAS crawling with local police, FBI agents, and federal marshals.

"If there's anything the FBI loves more than a kidnapping, it's a triple kidnapping," said Hank Gaines.

"What are you doing here?" I asked. "Aren't you just a little out of your jurisdiction?"

"Yeah, but not as much as Kim was when he went to Brooklyn with you."

"What makes you think he did that?"

"Because he's with you, and Cantrelli's headquarters in Bensonhurst is burning to the ground and every house on the block is going with it. Besides, I called Connie and she told me."

"You cheated," I said, walking toward the house.

"Yeah, that's right, O'Keefe. Now tell me what you're up to or I'll blow the whistle on you to the FBI boys. I know you called that pilot, Kenny, because he came in about twenty minutes ago and went up to the airstrip to preflight Jack's twin Beech. I know you made arrangements to be picked up in Albany by Kim Woo's brother because he called here and left a message. You don't have to go inside to pick it up. He says he'll be waiting for you at a small airport east of Troy in a place called Poestenkill. I already briefed Kenny. He knows the airport and the surrounding area."

"So, where is this leading, Hank?" I asked, my hand on the front door knob.

"I want to go with you. I want to be in on the action for once instead of just the clean up crew."

"Hank, you're mad! No, damn it, just leave it alone! It's my show and I don't want you or anyone else to get hurt."

"You don't have a choice, Billy. I already loaded my gear on the aircraft and I got my army Colt .45 and six extra clips."

"Let him come. We can use the extra hand where we're going," said Kim

So it was decided. We were a team. If things continued, we would end up an army, which was what we'd need to pull it off. I began to shake as the airplane took off, just like before in Nam when we would go on a mission. The difference then was, we were young and didn't know any better.

"The field we're going into has a short runway, power lines and a hill on the north, trees to the south," Kenny yelled over the roar of the engines. "It's in a low lying area but it's a hard surface runway, and there's a telephone with a Coke machine outside the hangar, not a bad little place to land. I called ahead and asked the airport manager to leave the runway lights on. I'll drop you fellows off and be back in about an hour. My partner, Butch Wakowski, is bringing our chopper up. If you need a lift out, just call on the radio. You got flares so I'll be able to find you. Any questions?"

"Always nice to have air support," quipped Hank.

"We do our best," said Kenny, as he leveled off.

"The hunting camp is somewhere up on the mountain east of the town," said Kim. "I don't know how much space there is for landing a chopper, but if we need you, we'll call on guard, 121.5."

"Okay, 121.5 it is. That'll freak out Albany tower but they could probably use some excitement anyway," Kenny said.

The trip only took twenty-five minutes and it was fully dark when we approached the airport from the south. Visibility was unlimited, so we could see the lights of cars on the highways and houses in the small towns all over the area. The lights of Albany glowed west of the Hudson River on our left and Kenny pointed out the rotating green/white beacon of Albany airport as he let down for our landing east of the river. Kim's brother was waiting as we taxied off the runway to the apron in front of the hangar.

"You guys didn't waste any time," he said. He was shorter, younger, and thinner than Kim with the same bemused smile. A carbon copy of his older sibling.

"This is my brother, John," said Kim. "He's smaller and younger then me but he's a lot meaner."

John shook hands, a big smile on his face. He didn't look mean but I noticed he was well built and very strong as he loaded our gear into the back of his 4X4. He had the same catlike movements as his older brother. He carried a Special Forces knife, similar to mine but much newer. Probably bought it from a magazine or a surplus store, I thought.

"Where did you get the knife, John?" I asked.

"My CO gave it to me in Iraq. I left mine behind in the desert."

"Iraq, Special Teams?" I asked.

"Yeah," and he walked away.

We climbed into the 4X4 and John drove through the small town of Poestenkill, stopping dutifully for a stop sign at a four-way intersection. He put on his blinker, turned right and started up the mountain on a narrow, bumpy tarred road lined either side by pine and oak trees.

"This place was named for the river," John explained as we bumped along. "Poestenkill is a small creek that runs down the mountain and through the town. The name is Dutch and 'kill' means river or waterway in Dutch. Funny thing about where we're going. These mountains flatten out on top so there are a lot of small ponds and lakes and most of the area is pine swamp so thick you can't even walk in it."

"Cantrelli's hunting lodge is back in the forest about half way over the mountain," he continued. "On the other side of the ridge is the town of Berlin, near the New York-Massachusetts border. Most of the settlers in that area were Germans who came over in the late 1800's. Some of them still speak a sort of German dialect and they don't mingle much with outsiders. Cantrelli has capitalized on the closed attitude of these people. He pays off some of the locals to keep them quiet. They don't like outsiders so they keep to themselves, and he does pretty much as he wants and nobody says anything."

John slowed for a curve and turned left onto a smaller dirt lane, lined with spruce and overgrown by princess pine. We traveled slowly, working our way over tree stumps and rock outcroppings into an area of large oak and maple trees.

"I don't see any swamp," said Hank.

"High ground, stick around, it gets better," John said.

We started down hill, the wheels skidding sideways on the leaves and mud, the vehicle tilting menacingly. John spun the steering wheel and we plunged between two large pines, the tires slipping and sliding downhill into a muddy hole at the bottom of the slope were we went in up to the floor.

"Darn it! We're off the road," said John.

"How much further?"

"Maybe half a mile."

"That's good. Don't try to get it out. They'll hear us." I said.

We hiked in almost total darkness. After falling twice, I suggested that John use a penlight to help us along. He led us around a small lake to within a hundred yards of the entrance of the camp where we hunkered down and discussed strategy. It was agreed that John and Kim would go forward and "neutralize the guard" at the front gate. Hank and I would work our way around and cut through the fence, and we would meet on the other side, so to speak.

Stars shone brightly through occasional openings in the trees but it was pitch dark in the woods. The smell of the princess pine and swamp spruce was overpowering, as were the mosquitoes and the croaking of the frogs in the marshy swamps surrounding the lake and camp. Hank was in worse shape then I was, so I found myself waiting for him as we crept through the thick undergrowth to the fence. John was right, it was a cattle fence with the standard five by six inch spaces formed by spot welding twelve-gauge wire. The top wire of the fence was nailed to a row of 2"x6" planks suspended along the tops of the cedar posts. The wire was rusty and the wood was covered by moss. I cut through the fence with ease and we made our way back to the gate. The Woos had the guard hog-tied and gagged.

"Neat job, huh, O'Keefe? He didn't even know we were here. We just crawled up behind him and grabbed his arms, knocked his feet out from under him and bang, on the ground," John whispered. I grabbed his arm and led him over into the shadows of the bushes.

"Listen to me, son! That's a Navy Seal and the weapon next to him is a Stoner-50, one of the most powerful and awesome handheld weapons made. It carries one hundred fifty rounds in that drum and more in the belt around his neck. You're lucky to be alive. From now on, don't play football with these guys. They're killers and if you don't take them out, they'll come back to haunt you. Do you hear me? Leave no survivors!"

"Man, you act like this is a war. What are you, some kind of a fanatic or something?" asked John.

"Boy, this is a war!" I grabbed him by the collar. "They've already killed innocent people. They destroyed homes and a general store. If you're too squeamish to do this then leave, because when all hell breaks loose they'll try to kill all of us and I'm depending on you to shoot to kill."

"I'll be there when you need me." John stared me steadily in the eye with the look of a warrior.

"Okay, I believe you. Now follow me."

Kim said, "I'll take responsibility for that, O'Keefe. We didn't discuss rules of engagement. We should be all right, now."

"Sorry, I'm a bit on edge," I said.

Hank picked up the Stoner and the extra belts of ammo and took a Colt .45 from the hogtied Seal. Then he whacked him over the head with the butt of the Stoner.

"Insurance," he whispered.

"Good work," I said and led off along the fence staying clear of the light and open spaces.

A sparsely wooded no-man's land of trees about a hundred yards deep lay between the fence and the camp. The main cabin, a one-story log structure about forty feet long with lights around the roof was set against a line of tall pines on the far side of an open clearing of about an acre. A guard sat outside the front door, smoking a cigarette. I led the way to the right around the clearing and came to a helicopter. It looked like the one I brought down that night at Jack's estate. A guard sat on the ground beside the left main tire.

We were on the east side of the clearing, still in view of the front of the cabin where the other guard sat smoking, about fifty yards from the helicopter. It was an impossible set up, yet we had to take out all the exterior guards or we would never make it. Just as I had decided to do it myself, Kim knelt beside me and pointed to the guard, then to himself. I nodded and watched as he crawled into the opening on all fours and then began to belly crawl very slowly up behind the right tire of the helicopter.

He watched carefully, making certain the guard at the cabin was turned away. Then he angled up behind the man sitting on the ground, pulled his knife, put his left hand around the man's face, rapped him hard on the back of the head, and then very carefully shoved the knife into the left side of the guard's back and moved the blade around, twisting and turning in order to do as much damage as possible. He leaned the man up against the tire and left him, a dying decoy making everything look normal. After that I had no doubts about Kim Woo or the rules of engagement.

We left Hank there for cover and made our way around the back of the cabin where there was total darkness. John and Kim each went around one side of the cabin to the front to take out the guards. I checked the back windows. They were nailed shut with heavy wire mesh over the outside frames. The room on the left was a bathroom, while the one in the middle was a utility room full of firewood, and hunting clothes hanging on wooden pegs. The window on the right was the prize.

Inside, in the dim reflection of a single light bulb, sat Walter St. Onge surrounded by my three offspring. I pulled my knife and tapped lightly on a pane of glass. At first there was no response. Then Timothy looked up and saw my face. I froze but he handled it like a real pro. He quietly turned to the others, put his finger to his lips and signaled for absolute quiet. Then he spoke and pointed to the window, all the while cautioning Jonathan and Samantha to remain quiet. Walter came to the window, grinned and gave the thumbs up. Then he indicated the nails and I showed him the knife.

Kim and John came back with two AK-47s, and we set about pulling the wire mesh off the window frame. We cut the wood away from the nails and pulled them out with the pliers I had purchased earlier. I unscrewed the shim plates in the frame and removed the windows.

Walter handed the kids out one at a time.

"See?" said Jonathan. "I told you he'd come."

"You were just guessing," sneered Samantha.

"No," said Timothy. "A promise is a promise." He looked at me with moistening eyes and said, "You promised to come if we needed you, and you came." He threw his arms around me and held tightly.

The children were in their pajamas with no shoes, just as they had been taken. I noticed Timothy had a bruise and a lump on his right temple. He'd taken a pretty good hit. Walter St. Onge wore a pair of boxer shorts, a T-shirt and no shoes. He was halfway out the window when someone raised the alarm in front of the cabin, and just then Hank cut loose with the Stoner.

"We've had it," Kim said running for the corner of the cabin.

"Call Kenny and tell him we're on our way out," I said to John.

I grabbed Jonathan by the armpit and swung him up on my shoulders. I scooped up Samantha with my left arm and Timothy with my right, started back into the darkness of the woods and began to work my way toward Hank's position. Kim and John were right behind us.

"Hank's got them bottled up but not for long," yelled Kim. "Let's move it." He grabbed Timothy from me and started to run.

John took Samantha and Walter pulled up the rear hobbling along in his bare feet. By the time we reached Hank, who was firing from behind a large pine tree, there was scattered fire from the cabin.

"Man, this Stoner is an awesome piece of work," yelled Hank.

"Yeah and they got more of them than we do, so conserve your ammo and keep your head down," I yelled.

Just then the windows of the cabin erupted with automatic gunfire. We hit the dirt and tried to find places to hide. Samantha began to scream and Jonathan cried. I told Timothy to stay down in the depression I'd put him in behind a tree and I crawled forward and commenced firing at the windows of the cabin with the Glock. The fire from the cabin was heavy but they hadn't figured out where we were, so they were firing on all quadrants.

"I think I got one," yelled Hank. "They're firing everywhere. Maybe we should bug out of here and head for the 4X4."

"They'll run us to ground if we try it," I yelled. "We've got to get some help. There's still a fully armed squad in there and they've got a back door."

"You didn't plan this out very well, did you O'Keefe?" yelled Hank, as he reloaded his Stoner-50. "You got us in, now get us out of here!"

"John, any word from Kenny and the chopper?" I yelled. The fire from the cabin was increasing.

"No, nothing. I'll keep trying."

"Keep firing…Look out! Somebody's over there in the trees," yelled Kim.

Before I could say anything, he was gone with John behind him. I crawled back to Timothy and pulled him to me.

"We gotta get out of here," I yelled. "We're in big trouble!"

CHAPTER TWENTY-SEVEN

I GATHERED THE OTHER TWO children and with Walter's help moved back into the trees. I found a fallen pine tree and put the children in the hole left by the roots. Just then I heard it, the beat of helicopter blades coming our way. I pulled the flare gun, fired into the air and waited as John came ducking toward us.

"Man, they're spreading out into those trees either side of the cabin. If we don't get outta here soon, we're dead meat."

The helicopter came closer and I fired another flare. Kenny's voice came crackling over the radio.

"I see the flare and I see the opening in front of the cabin but there's gun fire all over. Where are you?"

I grabbed the radio and yelled. "We're pinned down in the trees south of the cabin. Enemy in the cabin and woods each side of cabin. Area is hot...repeat, area is hot, over." The reply was a classic.

"Roger, dodger, baby. Standby for a delivery and keep your heads down!"

"What did he say?" asked John.

"Get Hank and Kim out of there. Tell them INCOMING!"

"Shit!" John crawled off and I heard him yelling.

The chopper came overhead and circled the area once. The firing from the cabin was reduced but there were several shooters in the trees either side of the building. Oddly enough the lights were still on outside. The inside lights were out and I could see shooters at each of the three front windows. I counted four more in the trees outside. Kenny called again.

"Fire another flare so I can see your position," he said over the radio.

I did and suddenly the chopper came alive. There was an M60 mounted in the open door of Kenny's helicopter, and someone was manning it, sweeping the cabin and surrounding woods with a vengeance. The chopper made two full circles of the area, pouring a withering fire into the cabin and trees. I fired two flares into the cabin just to help. Kenny ceased firing and circled once more before setting down. As he circled the last time, two figures emerged running toward the idle helicopter on the ground. They were just about to climb into the front seats when Hank let loose with his Stoner and cut them down. Kenny landed his helicopter and we ran for it. A short man in overalls crouched in the open cargo door, manning the M60. He kept scanning the area, firing as we loaded up.

"We can only handle four," yelled Kenny. "This is Butch, my partner. I'll come back and pick up the rest of you. The FBI is on their way up here, so I wouldn't stay around too long."

We helped the children on board and Walter said he'd stay but I told him to go. I had some mopping up to do.

"Besides, Walter," I yelled, "you look ridiculous with no pants on." He got into the chopper without any more arguments.

We policed the area and found several wounded and dead in the trees. There were only two Navy Seals accounted for, the one we had tied up and one in the woods. The rest were Latinos wearing lizard shoes and belts. We checked the two that Hank had cut down as they ran for the Italian helicopter. One was a pilot, the keys for the ignition switch of the helicopter still clutched in his right hand.

"The other one is Senator Cantrelli," said Hank. "He's still alive but not for long. That Stoner nearly cut him in half."

"That's poetic justice," I said. "Kenny's brother got it the same way only it was an AK-47. Let's have a look," I said.

Hank was right. Cantrelli was a mess. He was conscious and fully lucid but he was going fast.

"Cantrelli, can you hear me?" He looked at me and smiled.

"O'Keefe! I might have known..."

"Who's the head of SARTXE? Tell me now and clear your conscience. Who's SARTXE?"

"Up yours...jerk..." He was bleeding from his nose, mouth, and ears and the rest of him was a mess.

"Is Sontaigm the head of SARTXE? You can tell me. He's through anyway, just like you and your son."

"What? What about Vic...Wha' you do to 'em?"

"He's through, Cantrelli. You lost and Vic is dead."

"No...I told him...get away. He's gone..."

"Is Sontaigm the head of SARTXE?"

"Nah...Nah." He shook his head. "You aren't getting' anything outta me. This isn't workin'..."

"It worked on your bodyguard, Sal Pinucci. He spilled his guts before he went. He wanted a priest...how about you, Victor? Do you want a priest? You want to clear your conscience?"

"Pinucci...Him 'n Stanley. They're SARTXE...is my son okay?"

"He's dead," I lied. "It's all over, Victor. Is Pinucci the head of SARTXE?"

"What's the diff..." He mumbled and his head slumped down.

Kim came out of the burning cabin with a Stoner in his hands. "We've got three Stoners but only two Navy Seals. There are two bodies in the woods over there and two more positions where someone was firing. One was a Stoner and the other an AK-47. I'd say we've got two loose shooters out there and they're armed."

"We'd better mop up and get outta here," said Hank.

"Let me check something out first," I said. Bending down I opened Cantrelli's coat and checked the inside pockets.

There it was, the report stolen from Jack Sullivan's safe, marked Top Secret, riddled with holes and soaked with blood. I took it and headed for the cabin, but before I reached the front door John came around the corner pushing a very reluctant and disoriented young man ahead of him. The resemblance was striking. It was Victor Cantrelli Junior, the Senator's son.

"Look at what I found," said John. "He was out there in the woods leaning against a tree, talking to himself. Looks like he got grazed in the head. I didn't think you would want me to kill him before you got a chance to talk to him, so I brought him in. What do you want to do with him?"

"We could shoot him, right O'Keefe? You said take no prisoners." said Hank laughing.

"Yeah, hell! Shoot him," I said, grinning.

"Wait...wait..." Junior started to cry. "Don't shoot me, please. We didn't hurt anybody...please. We just did like we were told." Tears mixed with blood from his wound streamed down his face.

"Who's the head of SARTXE. Who's calling the shots?"

"I don't know. Where's my father?"

"He's dead, Vic baby, and so are you if you don't answer me."

"Oh God, no...no...it wasn't supposed to happen this way."

I grabbed him by the throat and slammed him against the cabin wall. "SARTXE, slime ball. Who is the head of SARTXE?"

"It's Pinucci. Him and dad, I think…"

"What about Sontaigm? Where does he fit?"

"He was just the broker. Dad and Pinucci funneled the money to him to invest. He used it to buy his way into politics."

"Whose idea was it to strip the drug cartels of their money?"

"That was Sontaigm. He sold the President some baloney about tracing drug monies through electronic transfers. He didn't tell the President the real plan was to steal the money. Sontaigm took it the rest of the way on his own. Forged the report and all…"

"But the President called Jack Sullivan, right? That complicated things so you had to get the report back before Jack saw it, right?" I said.

"Yeah, and then there was you. For some reason everybody was afraid of you..." He looked at me with glazed eyes. "They were right weren't they? For an insurance investigator you should have been a Navy Seal."

I heard the chopper returning. "Tie him up and let's get out of here," I said, tossing the clothesline to Hank.

I took a quick look inside the cabin and came back outside. It wasn't a pretty sight. The M60 machine gun had devastated the place and everyone in it. The flares had started the fire which was doing the rest. We boarded the chopper and it lifted off with Kenny at the controls and his partner, Butch, beside him in the co-pilot's seat. We broke out the box of Snickers and celebrated as we skimmed the tree tops going down the mountain.

"The FBI is at the airport," said Kenny, "so I'm going to make a quick stop at the far end of the runway. I'll turn the door away from the hangar so they can't see that M60 mounted back there. Then I want to get this baby back to the hangar and hide that gun before someone sees it."

"Hey, can you take these Stoners and AK-47s with you too?" asked Kim. "I'll pick them up later." Kenny nodded.

"Man I don't know where you got that M60 but it sure was a welcome sight when you cut loose with it. I thought we were goners before that," said Hank.

"Butch is a gun collector," Kenny yelled over the engine noise. "He's even got a permit for it."

We started letting down over the side of the mountain into the valley. As we came in over the hangars, I saw that there was a traffic jam of police cars and ambulances all around the buildings.

They were on us en masse almost before Kenny got off the ground, pointed south over the trees. Hank stayed with the chopper, taking his Stoner with him. Kim and John stood either side of me as a veritable army of FBI agents, federal marshals, state police and local cops came charging at us, all armed to the teeth.

They surrounded us with weapons drawn like hunters who'd just treed a possum. Agent Corsini stepped through the crowd, followed by a man in a dark blue suit, white shirt, and dark tie.

Corsini said, "O'Keefe! This is Assistant Director Mingus and he has ordered me to arrest you for interfering in a federal investigation. Put out your hands and come quietly." He took a pair of handcuffs out of his pocket and reached for my arm. I put out my hands but he never cuffed them.

"Drop dead, worm!" I said, and I hit him as hard as I could right between the eyes.

CHAPTER TWENTY-EIGHT

THE DUST DIDN'T SETTLE for a good twenty minutes. Kim Woo demonstrated his advanced karate, Tae Kwon Do and street fighting techniques as did his brother, John. I did a few kicks and gouges, a couple of knee crunches and a poke or two to the eyes, and when we were through, there were a couple dozen FBI agents and federal marshals flat on the ground.

Why, you may ask? I suppose the devil made me do it. Maybe I was just angry and I didn't feel like being arrested by a bureaucratic jerk that'd been pronging my ex-wife and was guilty of letting my children be kidnapped. Maybe I just hadn't gotten all the fight out of my system. Whatever! It felt good, and even though the three of us ended up in the dirt with about forty agents and marshals on top of us it was still worth it, even though I would be sore for a month.

We spent the rest of the night explaining ourselves and by daybreak we were "free to go". The children had already been returned to the estate to comfort their mother who was reported to be somewhat distraught. Jack and Judith Sullivan were flying home. Walter St. Onge was on his way home with a new pair of pants provided by an FBI agent from Detroit. Agent Corsini was relieved of duty and Agent Thomas' citation for bravery had been canceled.

Agents were on their way to the White House with the Director of the FBI to meet with the President and then take Samuel Sontaigm for a ride "downtown". Admiral Rassmussen and Ambassador Kitterage received similar visits after it was confirmed the President had not authorized the transfer of a Navy Seal team and that Sontaigm had altered the Top Secret report. Pinucci and Stanley were considered lesser players from a federal viewpoint and would receive attention later. John Delmar sang like a canary when he was threatened with arrest, and they couldn't write it down fast enough.

John Woo led an expedition of agents and marshals up the mountain, over the hill and through the swamps to Cantrelli's hunting camp. A report came back that there had been a hell of a battle and Senator Cantrelli was dead. A couple of Navy Seals were found tied and gagged, and one was Cantrelli Junior. Both were singing their hearts out after being threatened with treason. Assistant Director Mingus was not happy about the way things turned out.

"If I had my way, you three and that helicopter jockey would fry in the federal penitentiary," he said.

The problem, however, was Agents Corsini and Thomas. The big stink of it all was their neglect of duty, plus the embarrassment the Agency would suffer if the press got hold of the real story. I promised this would happen if Kim, John and I were not released. I think we had some help from Jack Sullivan and Kim's contacts in the Pentagon helped too. Kenny flew us back to the estate in Jack Sullivan's twin Beech and I fell asleep as soon as we were airborne. I avoided their mother, and after a brief reunion with the kids I took a quick shower, scrounged up a change of clothes, and talked Kim Woo into a ride.

"I've got some unfinished business and a few more laws to break, Kim. Are you game?"

"I'm in it until the fat lady sings. Besides, if I go back to work now, I'll probably get charged with arson, first degree murder, theft of top secret government documents and consorting with a known lunatic, that's you."

"That's me." I agreed.

"Right, and I'm too young to spend the rest of my life in prison."

We took the Tappan Zee Bridge to the Garden State Parkway, south to I-80 to Fairfield, a town west of Paterson. We stopped for a late lunch at a Burger Hut and I briefed Woo on my plan.

"You don't have to come along if you don't want to, Kim. This one is personal and I can't guarantee I'll behave myself this time."

"You mean like in Brooklyn? Can it get any worse?"

"It could. I've been known to lose it from time to time."

"Yeah, I know. Like punching out an FBI agent in the middle of a joint FBI-Federal Marshal reunion. I was there. Whatever possessed you to do that, O'Keefe? You started a riot."

"I don't know. It seemed right at the time. You didn't seem to have any problem joining in."

"Oh no! I had no choice, it was them or us."

"So you enjoyed it?"

"Yeah, right up to the point where the other fifty guys jumped on top of me and I swallowed a pint of dirt. Look at these bruises."

We had a good laugh and everyone in the restaurant looked at us like we were crazies. Little did they know! We finished our hamburgers and I made a phone call to confirm the location of my target.

'Mr. Pinucci was on his way home and would not be back in the office until tomorrow morning,' his secretary said. The address was not far away. We found the house; a modern brick colonial perched on a knoll overlooking the Passaic River on a small tarred, tree-lined road. We took up a position around a bend in the road where we could see the house and driveway. It was late afternoon.

"There he is. Drives a Mercedes 560SLX, nice car," said Kim.

"Crime pays," I said opening the door.

We cut across the lawn and caught him as he got out of his car. Woo spun him around, pushed him up against the car and frisked him coming up with a small .25 caliber Beretta automatic.

"What the hell do you think you're doin?" Then he spotted me. "YOU! O'Keefe, damn you! I'll have you shot for this."

"You already tried, buster, and it didn't work. You want to try again with this little pee shooter? Your brother tried with an M-16 and he's dead." I spun him around and punched him in the gut.

"Don't kill him here," said Woo with a wink.

"Maybe not now," I said. "If he doesn't cooperate, we do him later, okay?" I grinned.

"What do you want? Just tell me what you want," he gasped.

"We have business to conduct and we don't have much time, so cooperate and you might live. Don't cooperate and you're history.

They'll never find a single piece of you, understand?" I hit him again.

His head bobbed and we duck-walked him across the lawn and loaded him into the back of the car. Woo drove to the Jersey Mutual headquarters in Montclair. It was after hours and the parking lot was empty. The building, a standard modern cement-steel-beam four-story structure, was designed not to burn, but that was about its only good point. We entered a back door and took a private elevator up to the fourth floor where Pinucci had his plush executive offices.

"Don't try anything funny, Anthony. I don't care how many people I waste today. Actually, I'm below my quota for the week so go ahead and try something, I need the excitement," I said.

"You're crazy, O'Keefe. You'll never get away with this. There's people lookin' for you and they got your kids, so how can you even think of messin' around with me?"

"You don't know, do you jerk?" I said pushing him into his overstuffed leather swivel chair. "I got my kids! The only people looking for me want to give me an award for wasting a Navy Seal team and a bunch of Cubanos, plus one senator and a bunch of off-duty Chicago cops as well as the other slime buckets you sent after me. Now, I've got you to play with."

"Yeah, right, you're bluffin'. Nobody could do all that and live. You're just flappin' your chops. You're here to find out where they're keepin' your kids. Well, you're not getting it out of me, buster. I ain't talkin'." He tried to turn away.

I hit him in the face with my fist. His nose poured blood and his upper lip was split.

"Listen up, Anthony, and pay attention real good. We already hit the hunting camp in East Poestenkill last night. Cantrelli's dead and his son is in FBI custody singing his heart out. You are going to join one of them, it's your choice. That's why I'm here. You owe Jack Sullivan eighty-eight million dollars and you're going to return it to him, NOW! Do I make myself clear?" I slapped him hard.

"Up yours. Sullivan knew the risks. He was trying to hide his assets from the creditors in his real estate deals. How was I to know the economy was gonna tank? He took his chance and he lost."

"And now it's you're turn to lose, slime bucket. I don't need you,

Pinucci. I know how to send a telex. I can hack out a code and I can find your hidden bank accounts. I just thought maybe you would like to make it easy on yourself before the FBI gets to you." I slapped him across the face again.

"When they start on your files and private accounts they'll find everything. No matter what happens, Pinucci, you are through. SARTXE is through and Jack Sullivan will get his money back or you'll die a slow, painful death. You like to terrorize people but now it's your turn and then it's your family's turn. You thought you'd skip the country if anything went wrong, well forget it. The payoff is now, and I'm the grim reaper."

"You won't hurt my family. You're not the type."

"Think, friend, think what you did to my kids." "How did you like the way I did your brother and Cantrelli's headquarters in Brooklyn? Pretty neat, huh? Now it's your turn." I slapped him again. The realization showed in his face.

"Sal didn't deserve to die that way. You musta shot him in the back." Pinucci said, blood dripping down his chin.

"Sal was just like you, Anthony. He was stupid." Then I said to Kim, "Watch him."

I started to search the office but it was clean. There were very few personal items like family pictures, pens and pencils, gifts and awards. I've never known an insurance man who didn't have awards all over his desk and walls, and I've never known an Italian father and husband who didn't have family pictures and children's drawings for daddy all over his desk. Then I realized what was missing. There was no computer terminal. What, an insurance executive with no access to his business records?

A large chalkboard covered the inside wall. The outside wall was all windows, floor to ceiling. On the far wall from Pinucci's desk were book shelves with a small built in bar and a reading stand out front. A long table ran down the middle of the room. I noticed the windows were tracked for the extra heavy curtains rolled up at the top of the casings. I realized we were in a conference room. A series of floor to ceiling mirrors covered the wall behind the desk where Pinucci sat. It was very chic and very out of place.

"Open them up, Anthony!" I said.

"What? Whadaya mean?"

"The mirrors, dummy. Open them!"

"Up yours. I'm not doin' nothin' for you!"

I picked up a chair from the conference table and threw it at the center mirror. It shattered, revealing a room on the other side.

"Geeze Louise, O'Keefe," exclaimed Kim.

"You son-of-a..." yelled Pinucci.

He tried to stand up but Kim punched him in the jaw, knocking him unconscious back into the chair. I pushed the chair with Pinucci out of the way and pulled out the top middle drawer of the desk but found nothing. The right top drawer revealed a control panel with a variety of buttons and switches. I punched them all, turning the lights on and off, rolling the curtains down and up. One button turned on mood music and finally another opened the far left mirror into the inner office. There I found everything I wanted.

"Watch Pinucci while I cruise around in here."

I scouted the room, found a wall safe, some account books, and bank records. I switched on the computer terminal on the desk with Pinucci's family pictures all over it and typed in a few codes hoping to get lucky but no such luck.

"Hey Kim," I yelled, "is Pinucci awake?"

"Yo."

"Ask him where he keeps his code manual."

There was a pause. "He says 'stick it!' "

"Okay, ask him the combination to the safe."

Pause..."Same response."

"Okay, put him out again."

I waited until I heard the solid thwack, then I pulled out my .44 Magnum, stood about ten feet from the safe, aimed a bit low at the dial and squeezed off a round. The door buckled and bounced off the safe, rolling across the rug and against an outside window. Like my son, Jonathan, would say, the .44 Magnum is a 'wicked, awful, awesome' weapon.

"Ouch. Geeze," Kim yelled. "Give me some warning, will ya?"

"Sorry."

The code manual was in the safe. It looked current so I went to the computer terminal and began to play the game. I'd used the same system for years when I worked for State Mutual. Before long I found an account protected by Pinucci's personal executive code. My search was over. I diddled and doodled around with the computer until I had a lock on the location of Jack Sullivan's funds. They'd been transferred to an offshore bank in the Grand Cayman Islands some four months previously, and then to a Swiss bank.

I spent the next hour moving around inside Jersey Mutual's accounts, copying what was interesting and useful. I used Pinucci's personal code to do everything and then I deleted some key items the programmers would be looking for when they came to work. I was tempted to insert a virus to destroy the whole system, but there were a lot of policyholders who'd be hurt, so I restrained myself, at least for the moment. When I had everything I needed, I went back into the conference room where Kim was still watching Pinucci.

"Anthony, baby," I said. "You've been a very bad boy." He looked at me with glazed eyes as he held a wad of tissue paper stuffed up against his bloodied nose. "You took a lot of money from innocent unsuspecting people and you hid it in different foreign banks. Then you put your company into receivership with the state and asked the taxpayers to make good on the bogus losses."

"Up yours, you can't do nothin' to me, O'Keefe. This isn't East Harbour. You can't just walk in here and mess around the way you did there."

"I got news for you, Pinucci, I can do what I darned well please and there is nothing," I slapped him hard across the face," and I repeat, nothing you can do about it."

I was starting to feel nasty. Anthony Pinucci was a snake. He tried to kill Connie and me. He had my children and Walter St. Onge kidnapped and stole Jack Sullivan's money, not to mention a lot of other people's money. I could go on listing his bad points but it no longer mattered. I didn't need a list to justify what I was going to do. I had made a decision, right then, about Anthony's future. Enough was enough! It was time to end the insanity.

"Kim, why don't you go out, start the car and wait for me? I have some sweeping up to do here. No sense in leaving a mess."

"This doesn't sound too good, O'Keefe. Why don't we just turn him over to the FBI and let them do the rest. Like you said, the FBI is good at documenting evidence."

"They are but they're lousy at prosecuting white collar crime, and trying to tie him into the SARTXE conspiracy is likely to backfire. Conspiracies are hard to prove, and this slime has a lot of money, that can buy lawyers and protection and maybe even a new life in another country under a different name.

"I guess I let myself in for this, didn't I," said Kim, looking out the picture windows at the setting sun.

"In a way, yes."

"I could stop you," he said.

"You could try but it wouldn't be worth it. I'd come back."

"I'm younger than you."

"Yes, but are you meaner?"

"Good point," he said walking slowly out of the room, a changed young man with much to think about.

CHAPTER TWENTY-NINE

PINUCCI TRIED TO STAND up. "You can't do this, O'Keefe."

I hit him over the head with the magnum barrel and he slumped back in the chair. I thought I might have hit him too hard but his pulse was still strong so I wheeled the chair over in front of the windows and turned it so he was facing out, looking west at the sunset. I went into the office and retrieved a bundle of cash that he had in the safe for traveling money. He wouldn't need it for the kind of traveling he was going to do. I was feeling mean now and all I wanted was to have done with it.

I found three of those table candles behind the bar, you know the ones in the little red globes filled with wax and a wick in the middle and they're harder than Hades to light. I got them going, and placed them on the conference table, one at either end and one in the middle for equal distribution. I turned on the mood music, checked Pinucci's pulse again, grabbed a magazine off the bar and went out, leaving the conference room door open behind me. The stairs were halfway down the hall so I tore the magazine in half and stuffed it under the stairwell door to keep it open. I did the same to the basement stairwell door, five stories down with the other half.

Fire is the one big threat that all insurance companies fear. So, with the help of fire inspectors and building codes, all modern buildings are built to standardized fire codes with non-burnable materials.

However, they overlook some other hazards an arsonist can exploit.

I'd noticed some gas meters on the side of the building when we came in. So, leaving the basement door to the stairwell open, I followed the gas pipes to the furnace. A two and a half inch pipe about eight feet long, probably left over from previous repairs, stood in the corner. I took it and flipped the emergency switch on the furnace to "OFF", killed the pilot light and set about breaking the gas pipe by levering the salvaged eight foot piece between the main gas pipe and the main water intake pipe on the back of the furnace. I had to put my full weight into and it took some straining and pumping but the pipe finally broke and gas began to pour out, making a loud whistling sound.

If it worked, it would be a long shot at best, but another thing about modern buildings is, they're airtight, so I could be sure the gas would eventually rise up the stair well without seeping out of the building. Natural gas is not as volatile as gasoline but it rises instead of settling like gasoline fumes do and the volume of gas spewing out of that broken pipe would eventually do the job. I went up to the front door on the first floor and found the guard with his back turned, reading a newspaper and a TV blaring out a rerun of MASH. He never knew what hit him. I made certain he was all right and carried him out on the front lawn. Kim Woo was sitting in his car around back of the building, chewing gum.

"Do I dare ask?" he said.

"He's still alive. I left him with some things to think about and I'm sure he'll see the light. Let's get going. I need a drink."

We ran into heavy traffic and a long backup at the Lincoln Tunnel. Manhattan was one big traffic jam. I offered to grab a cab but Kim insisted on driving me all the way to the CIC building. We got a hero's welcome from Kate and Walter. Connie let me know she was glad to see me, too.

We relaxed with wine and cheese while we watched the evening news. I was appropriately shocked to see the Jersey Mutual building burning like a roman candle on the TV screen.

"Anthony Pinucci, president and CEO, was killed by an explosion which blew him out the picture windows of his office. He must have been sitting at his desk because his chair went with him. The guard was interviewed but he didn't remember anything before or after the fireworks," said the announcer. "Evidently, he was blown out of the building also and was found unconscious on the front lawn."

We introduced Kim to Arturo's Restaurant and indulged in a night of gluttony. It turned out that Kim was a connoisseur and had dined on real Italian cuisine many times during his travels in the mother country. He pronounced Arturo's cooking to be the finest of the real thing, even down to the pimientos and olives in the antipasto. After the food, Arturo's fiddle and the dancing came out again. Kim surprised us by doing a real Italian peasant dance with Arturo's wife, Mamie. Then he shifted to a classic Viennese waltz with Kate.

"We better watch this guy, he's too good to be true." said Walter.

"You wouldn't have thought that way if you saw him in action at that hunting camp," I said and I told Walter about the guard leaning against the helicopter skid.

"Man oh man...he's as bad as you are, O'Keefe."

"Not really, he wanted Pinucci alive for the FBI."

Walter looked at me, an expression of surprise on his face. "So the fire at Jersey Mutual wasn't an accident. My God, that's murder. How can you live with that?" he asked.

"Yes it is, Walter and I can live with it only because I have to. Think what would happen if we waited for the FBI to investigate, and think about the Insurance Commissioner in New Jersey. Do you think we would see any movement there?"

"Hell, no! The insurance commissioners in these states are all tied in with the insurance companies, especially in Jersey." "Yes, and then there's the SEC, the IRS, the ICC and the Banking Commissioner. Have I named anyone that you think might do anything effective where Pinucci is concerned?" I added.

"No," he said, looking troubled.

"You see, Walter," I said, the noise of Arturo's fiddle overriding our conversation, "Samuel Sontaigm, Ambassador Malcome Kitterage, Admiral James Rassmussen, Senator Victor Cantrelli, the Navy Seal team, the Cuban mercenaries - they're all on the federal level where the FBI has an interest. Pinucci is a local hood, so he's subject to state agency jurisdiction, and what state has the worst track record for control of insurance companies outside of Texas?"

"New Jersey," I suppose, Walter said, reluctantly.

"Right, so Pinucci had no fear of what might happen to him. As long as he stayed in New Jersey he was protected, and if anything happened beyond Jersey he was protected by SARTXE, and if anything happened beyond that, he had millions stashed in the Grand Caymans and Switzerland. I don't know exactly how much, but it appears to be about nine hundred million in all from what I saw in his secret accounts."

"Good grief, that much?"

"Probably a lot more and we may never know how much John Stanley, president and CEO of State Mutual, and the others have hidden away. They've been doing this for a long time and they probably kept separate accounts."

"You think Stanley has an equal amount then?"

"It's something to pursue in the future. So, there you have it. Those are the alternatives. Call it murder. Call it expediency. Call it whatever you want. My old CO in Vietnam, Captain Matthew Thornton always said, 'If the bastard deserved to die, then it's not murder. That's Texas justice'. "

Walter thought a few moments, the music and dancing still going on behind us. "The problem is, Billy, this isn't Texas, it's New York."

"True, Walter, and maybe that's why SARTXE operated here and not in Texas. So what do you think? Can you live with it?"

"Yes...Ahh, yes, I can live with it now that you've explained it. It's hard to believe that such people even exist, but now that you explain it, I see what you mean and yes I guess I can live with it. Good grief, even the enemy in Viet Nam wasn't as bad as these people. At least there, you got what you expected. These people, this SARTXE, damn! They were all supposed to be upright citizens, good guys, respected businessmen, politicians, diplomats, policemen, soldiers, respected members of society. Hell! They are the enemy!"

"You finally understand," I said. I had another convert.

CHAPTER THIRTY

"ARE YOU COUNTING YOUR body parts again, Billy?"

"Noooo...my head hurts too much to count."

"Oh, too bad. Did Tiger drink too much Chianti last night?"

"Ahhhh...something like that. Where are we?"

"Walter's penthouse, remember? You led the charge up the stairwell to the tenth floor before we all died and had to take the elevator the rest of the way. You were magnificent, O'Keefe. You were superb." Connie purred in my ear.

"Oh, how come I don't remember how much fun I was?"

We had breakfast and made ready to leave. Walter came into the living room, a telex in his hand and a look of dismay on his face.

"Bill, I just received this confirmation of a transfer of funds to a numbered bank account in the Grand Cayman Islands for eighty-eight million dollars. You know anything about it?"

"Like I said, Walter. I spent some time playing around with Pinucci's computer. You can ask Jack Sullivan where he wants his money. Just don't let the old fool put it all in one place again. Tell him my usual fee is ten percent, but I made an exception in his case because he's family.

Oh yes, one other thing. Here are two CDs you should find helpful. One is just some information I found while messing around in Jersey Mutual's computer. I copied it so you would see how they covered their tracks and washed the money out of their accounts. The other CD was in Pinucci's safe and it contains his entire personal file and accounts on all his SARTXE dealings. Think of it for a moment, Walter. This is his personal working disk. You'll see where all the money went and how he did it. Do as you wish about returning the money to its rightful owners."

"Wow! You really found all that on this disk?"

"Yes and here is his personal log and current code book. You won't need anything else."

We said our goodbyes and Kim drove us back to the estate where Jack and Judith Sullivan were waiting for us.

"William, I am so glad you're all right." Judith was at her best. "The children told us all about it. Connie, my dear, you look tired. It must have been a terrible ordeal. How are you?"

Jack looked the same. He never changed, except there seemed to be a sadness in his eyes, which I'd never seen before.

"I had a chat with the ladies," he said, "and they've agreed to let you take the children for a while. It wasn't easy. Judith and I will be returning to Pamplona. The bulls are all done and the tourists are gone, so things will be considerably quieter. We'll take Natalie with us. She's had a terrible time of it from what I hear." He paused, looked at me and then at Judith. "How can we ever repay you, Bill? I'll give you whatever you ask."

"I didn't do it for the money, Jack. Just take care of yourself and don't put your money all in one place again."

We laughed at that. Kenny offered to fly us back to Long Island with the children in Jack's twin Beech, and as we were walking up to the airstrip, Judith surprised me with another invitation.

"William," she said. "You and Connie must come to our Labor Day weekend bash. It's the end of the season. We'll have all sorts of interesting people here and of course we'll end it all with the usual fireworks display. It will be better than ever."

"Sounds interesting," I said, "but this time I think I'll skip the fireworks, if you don't mind."

EPILOGUE

THINGS ARE QUIETER NOW. The children are back in school and living with their mother in Scarsdale. Jack and Judith Sullivan returned to their estate overlooking the Hudson River, with their money safely in a bank where thieves and robbers cannot break in and steal it. I visited Gerry Perkins when he got out of the hospital and told him he did good and reassured him that he'd be okay. He thanked me for saving his life and said he was glad to see me again. He seemed different and I knew what he was going through. Connie and I spend as much time together as possible and we go sailing when the weather and her schedule permit. Hank and Kim are back at their jobs and Walter St. Onge is talking about marrying Kate. Hank came to visit the other day.

"I've been busy with paperwork, Billy. Looks like this case is never gonna go away. The FBI doesn't like being made fun of and the Pentagon doesn't like security breaches. My boss doesn't like AK-47s and Helen's gonna divorce me if I don't retire. Man, I miss the good old days."

"What good old days, Hank? We were just green kids when we met on our way to Viet Nam and as far as I can see, nothing's changed except that we got older."

"Yeah, you're right. We're not any smarter than we were then, that's for sure and we're still doing the big boys' dirty work."

"But we're still doing it our way and that's what counts," I added.

"Except I get paid a lot less than you. Man, your ten percent of this case must have set you up for life. Wish I had a score like that."

"I didn't make that much on this one, Hank. At least you have a pension coming. All I got was the satisfaction of seeing the bad guys go down. If I don't get a real job before winter, I may have to move in with you."

"Fat chance. Helen's making noises about going to her sister's place in Florida for the winter. I think she's serious this time. I don't blame her. I lost it the other night...you know what I mean. I had a...well..."

"The ghosts came to visit again?"

"Yeah...it took a while before I calmed down and she really got ticked off. Hell, I can't tell her what it's all about. You know that."

"We've talked about this before, Hank. You gotta learn not to fight it. It gets worse if you fight it. You just have to hang on."

"The nights are the worst, you know? So what do you do that's so great and I don't?" He sat on the top step of the porch.

"Sometimes in the middle of the night the ghosts from the past come to visit. When it happens, I come out here to the front porch and sit in my Grandfather's old rocking chair. I stare into the darkness at the breaking surf and hold on until they go away. Of course, it doesn't happen as often as it used to since Connie came into my life."

"That's nice. You're lucky to have a woman like that who understands. I don't have a rocking chair and my house is five miles from Long Island Sound. When it happens, it's like I'm back there all over again in the jungles and Helen's no help. There are times when I don't know if I can live with it. What about you?"

"Yeah, I can live with the things I've done, but only because I have no choice. There are times I wish I wasn't so good at what I do. They took us as boys and taught us to do things nobody should have to do. Then they dropped us into the jungles and gave us on-the-job training. Nobody wants to hear about it so here we are, living in civilization, trying to survive in ways nobody understands. It's not easy and it never goes away...completely. That's why we have to keep in touch with the others, the ones who have gone through it like we have."

"Yeah, I think you've got a point there. I like that Kim Woo and his brother John. They are some really good guys. I hope we can keep in touch with them."

"I think we will, Hank. I think we will. There are still a lot of bad guys out there that need to be stopped and we're just the ones to do it."

"Just do me a favor, O'Keefe. Don't ask me to fly on anymore helicopters, okay?"

"Okay, Hank. Hey, wanna go get some breakfast at Gabby's Diner?"

"Only if you're buying. I left my wallet at home."

"No problem, I'm planning on scoring big on my next case. You can owe me. By the way, here's a little something I found laying around in Anthony Pinucci's safe." I handed him an envelope full of cash.

"Geeze, O'Keefe, I can't take this. It's dirty money. I could get put in jail for this and so could you."

"Not really, Hank. It's money that's unaccounted for and it's yours to use anyway you please. You could put a down payment on that house in Florida for Helen to retire in. She'd like that, wouldn't she?"

"There's enough here to buy the whole house. Are you nuts, man? How will I explain it to her?"

"Tell her you've been saving and it's all for her. She'll love it. Come on Hank, you keep saying you miss the action. This is part of it. This is the pay off. Were you worried about losing your job up there on the mountain when you cut loose with that Stoner-50?"

"No, of course not but what about Kim and John? What if they find out?"

"They're taken care of. I always take care of my friends."

"Okay, but if I go to jail, you gotta take care of my family."

"It's a deal. Let's go eat."

And that's how it was, folks. So, if you have a problem that nobody else can solve, give me a call. I get ten percent of what I recover. No recovery, no ten percent but be careful what you ask for because sometimes it's hard to tell the good guys from the bad and it's not funny when things go boom. People get hurt and lives can be changed forever.

THE END

ABOUT THE AUTHOR

Alistair Newton has lived in the New York area and writes out of personal knowledge. He is a graduate of an Ivy League college and a qualified commercial pilot with experience in the business world. He bares no resemblance to O'Keefe except that both of them enjoy flying, sailing and fishing and each one believes in justice for the little guy.